MEN OF TRANCE

SIDE GAME

BOOK TWO

I0608095

Published by F-Bomb Publishing
www.f-bombpublishing.com

OTHER BOOKS BY NICOLE

Men of Trance
Got Mine

Thizz Series
Thizz, A Love Story
Illusions of Ecstasy

Lunam Series
The Lunam Ceremony
The Lunam Deception
The Lunam Legacy

Novellas
The Excursion

Anthology
Cop Tales

Playlist

Beyond, *Leon Bridges*
Jealous, *Labrinth*
Dive, *Ed Sheeran*
Oh! So Quiet, *Bjork*
Broken, *Lovelytheband*
RIP, *Olivia O'Brien*
Fall for You, *Leela James*
I Feel Like I'm Drowning, *Two Feet*
The Broken Hearts Club, *Gnash*
Playinwitme, *KYLE (ft. Kehlani)*

Six years ago

Guys like me don't wait in line. It doesn't matter if I'm a few years shy of being here legally. My presence increases the worth and reputation of the club.

Neon palm trees cast a green glow over a crowd of impeccably dressed patrons waiting to have their thirst quenched inside of Oasis. I roll past them with Cookie beside me. She is a life-size Brat doll—big hair, lips, and hips. Walking with her increases my worth exponentially.

I hand the doorman my id, he pretends the twenty-five-year-old dork on the fake driver's license is the same person standing four inches taller than him. He barely glances at Cookie's fabricated identification.

"Have a good night," he says and opens the rope so we can enter.

The bass drop hits as we walk in, announcing our arrival. It wasn't planned, but when you look this good the world works in your favor.

Industrial sized fans whirl on opposite ends of an illuminated dance floor. An empty pool lies beneath the thick glass squares embedded into the ground. Oasis used to be a motel. Remnants of that time are littered around the club. Old sofas and desk chairs create make-shift lounge areas.

Cookie pushes between two guys at the bar. One of them smiles and offers his seat hoping he has a chance. Cookie thanks him, then waves me over. The guy is a few inches shorter than me and about twenty pounds overweight. With a little help from his friend, he could probably take me down. This thought crosses my mind when I step beside Cookie and take the guys seat.

"You're going to get me killed," I warn Cookie.

"Dying in defense of my honor is a great way to go." She kisses my cheek then waves the bartender over.

Being here with Cookie diminishes my chances of getting laid. Never bring sand to the beach. But I don't have a car and taking the bus to the club—not cool.

I order two Captain and Cokes.

"I don't want to get drunk." Cookie places a hand on her hip. "I'm driving.

"It's mostly coke," I clarify. "Just have one." Thankfully, Cookie is a cheap date. She hardly drinks and has a rule about eating in public. What little money I have is pilfered from my tuition account. Dad says college isn't for fun, it's for learning. Clearly, he's never been. Every dime I spend in the club is one less meal I eat when I return to school. It's worth it.

Cookie takes a small sip of her drink, careful not to disturb her lipstick. "I'm going to dance." she pushes away from the bar and walks away. Six dudes follow her to the dance floor.

If I wanted, I could hit that. Cookie is beautiful, but her personality needs serious contouring. I finish my first drink then order another. The club isn't fun unless you're buzzed. I take my second drink upstairs. The view of the dancefloor is better from there. I can keep an eye on Cookie while I look for the reason I came here tonight. The reason I've come here for the last three nights.

Her purple hair is easy to spot and just part of the reason she stands out in a crowd of hundreds. She's like one of those porch lights that lure bugs to their death. You know she's dangerous but you can't stay away. People jockey for position around her. Waiting for their chance dance in her glow. Everyone but me.

Watching from a distance isn't my style, she isn't my style, and I'm not hers. Cookie knows her from school and swears she's strictly into females. This fact doesn't prevent me from watching, fantasizing.

Her eyes glance up to the second floor. I swear she looks right at me. I look away and find Cookie waving her arms to get my attention.

"My drink?" she mouths.

Shit, I left it on the bar. It's probably been rufied by now. I head downstairs and order her another drink. I've already spent half the money in my pocket on two rounds. Even if Cookie didn't drive, I'd be stuck paying for her drinks because I'm the guy. Somehow, men set precedence when it comes to buying drinks. It'd be nice if that philosophy worked both ways. I'm confident every woman standing at this bar would dance with me, possibly fuck me. Not one will open her Coach wallet and buy my drink.

Someone places a hand on my shoulder, I turn ready to punch. I'm not cool with people touching me. Male or female. I'm a big proponent of personal space. The hand belongs to a guy I know from the gym.

"S'up, Rico?" We bro hug.

"Just chillin'." Rico points at Cookie a few feet away. "Is she with you? I thought I saw you walk in together."

Of course you did.

"No, we shared a ride." Cookie stops pouting when she notices Rico checking her out.

"Mind if I dance with her?"

"Please, take her off my hands." I give him Cookie's fresh drink.

"I owe, son." Rico saunters towards Cookie and I'm off the hook.

"Can I get a shot," I yell to the bartender.

"What do you want?"

"Uh, I don't know. Whiskey?"

"What kind?" He's annoyed.

"Makers Mark," someone says.

"Make it two."

It's her. The purple-haired chick.

"Hi." She stands beside me with a crazy cool grin. "I've seen you here before." She points upstairs. She's noticed me watching her. "I've never seen you dance."

"I'm not a dancer."

"Then why come to a club?"

"I guess I like the view."

Damn, that was smooth.

She smiles in appreciation of my quick wit.

I've never been this close to her. She's like a live wire, igniting everything around her.

The bartender places the shots on the bar.

"Eighteen."

I pull my wallet out and start counting the last of my dollars.

"It's on me." She tosses a twenty on the bar.

My chest does this weird thing where it gets tight and I feel like every hair on my arm is standing up.

"Thanks."

"My pleasure." She smiles. "What are we drinking to?"

"You bought the drinks, you tell me."

She processes for half a minute then lifts her shot.

"May we get what we want, what we need, and never what we deserve."

I smile despite the corniness of her toast and touch my plastic shot glass to hers. I hesitate when the smell of the brown liquid hits my nose. She tosses hers back and I follow. For three seconds I'm sure it's going to come back up and shoot all over her face.

She drops her shot glass on the bar.

"That was so bad."

"Why did you order it?"

"I heard someone order it in a movie and I thought it would sound cool."

"It was cool," I assure her as I grip the bar for support while my stomach decides what to do. "Except for the part where I almost puked on you."

She thumps her chest with her fist, then lets out a small burp. I look up incredulously and begin laughing.

"Come on." She tugs my arm. "I know a place with a way better view."

I follow her upstairs and onto the roof. The November air slaps me across the face. Not even alcohol can warm you in this cold. She skips ahead of me towards an old sofa. The brown material is ripped and stained. She plops down on it and pats the seat beside her.

"Won't your friends wonder where you are?" I carefully sit on the dirty cushion and imagine all the bodily fluids that have seeped into the material beneath my ass.

"What friends?"

"The people you came with."

"Who said I came with people?"

"You always have a posse on the dancefloor."

She smirks. "I don't know them. We're just sharing space together. Enjoying the music."

She rolls solo, another check in the right box. I can get down with a woman who doesn't need reinforcements.

"Are you and Cookie a thing?"

"No way."

"You're not sticking your hand in her jar?"

She's funny. I like that.

"We're just friends." I make myself crystal clear.

She shivers and hugs herself. Normally, I'd ask if she were cold, slide my arm around her, and make my move. I get the feeling my moves won't work on her.

"How old are you?" I like that she's controlling the conversation.

"Twenty-one. Obviously."

She leans away to get a better look at me. "Truth?"

"I don't know you well enough."

"To be honest?"

"Honesty requires trust. I trust like two people."

"So, you lie to ninety-eight percent of the people you meet."

"I didn't say that."

"Apparently, you don't plan on saying much."

I sound like an asshole. I don't want to be that guy.

"I'm eighteen for another eleven weeks." Disclosing my age feels like peeling a layer of skin from my face.

"Now was that hard?" Her mouth twists into a smile. "I just turned eighteen."

If I didn't know she graduated with Cookie, I would've guessed twenty. I like that she's unreadable. I'm not sure where to classify her.

A friend.

A fuck.

My future.

"What are you thinking right now?" She nudges me with her elbow. "You look very serious." She says the last bit in a baritone voice.

"Just wondering what your story is."

And where I will fit into it.

"Let's see," she sighs. "I just ended a two-year relationship but we're still cool. I think it's important to always remain friends." She glows when she speaks. "How can you hate someone you loved? It makes zero sense to me."

"Are you friends will all your exes?"

The jealous dude in me imagines a future where I have to play nice with her exes.

"You can tell about a person by their past relationships."

"I only have one real ex and I'm pretty sure she has a bounty on my head."

She laughs like it's a joke. "You don't expect me to believe a guy like you has one ex?"

"Commitment isn't something I strive for when I meet a girl."

Until now.

"Strictly F.W.B.?"

"Friends with benefits has its benefits."

"That is so me right now." She hold her fist out and I bump it.

If she wants to keep it casual, I'm down. I'll take whatever she wants to give.

"I want to be selfish for a change. Enjoy my freedom while I can."

"Is your freedom in jeopardy?" I look at her concerned, like I'm sitting beside a felon.

"Nothing like that."

The light surrounding her goes dark for a moment. I wonder how much of what she gives the world is a performance. I see a tiny bit of me in her.

I'm the guy who gives fake names and phone numbers. The guy with two Facebook accounts. Playing baseball, going to college, everything that makes me who I am is done to please someone else. I want her to know I'm a safe-zone. She can be herself around me.

"I go to school up north. I'm home on break. Honestly, I don't want to go back. I feel like it's such a waste of time."

"It's only a waste if you waste it." She surveys my outfit, my shoes. "If I were you, I'd take full advantage of a free education."

She unfairly judges me based on my appearance. I want to be offended, but I'm not. She's right. I have it easy, but my parents aren't rich. They struggle to pay my tuition. A fact my father will never let me forget.

"Do you go to school?"

She sits back and looks at the sky. "I'm going to be all I can be."

The city lights prevent us from seeing the stars, even on a clear night. My phone vibrates in my pocket. I pull it out and find a text.

"Is it Cookie?"

"It's a dude who sells fake ID's. He's on his way so I can buy one for a friend of mine."

"I thought Cookie was giving you a fifteen-minute warning." Her shoulder touches mine. "What happens if she decides to go home with someone? Will she let you drive her Mustang?"

"How did you know Cookie drove?"

"Uh, an educated guess?" She covers her face. "I might have asked Cookie about you." She drops her hands. "Only because I've seen you watching me from your little perch." She's animated. "Technically, you're the creepy one."

"I'm flattered." My ego grows exponentially.

"Quit acting like I'm the first girl to inquire about your status." I don't confirm or deny, that would be an asshole thing to do. I also don't want her to think she's on the level of any random chick.

This girl is next level.

"You're the first to surprise me. I didn't think you were into..."

"Dudes?"

"Yes."

"I'm into people. Especially, ones with a smile like yours." The compliment sounds like something I should say to her. The role reversal is a huge turn on. If I had a vagina, I'd be wet right now.

"You dress the part of an asshole, no offense."

"It's cool, I was going for asshole so you nailed it."

She regards me for a second before continuing. She's impressed. Not with my clothes or game. She likes me and it surprises her. That makes two of us.

"I can tell you're really a sweetheart. That's why I brought you up here. I knew it was safe. For me." She leans in close, her hand on my thigh. Her lips inches from my mouth. "You're the one who should be worried. You don't know what I'm capable of." She slips back into performance mode. The act is her safe-zone. It's also sexy as fuck.

I want to grab her by the back of the head and pull her mouth to mine. Kissing will lead to fucking. I want more than a dirty romp on this roof. Then I'll just be the guy she fucked on the roof of Oasis. That isn't the story I want to write.

"I'm not normally pursued," I say in my sexy voice. "Usually I do the chasing."

"And let me guess, I'm supposed to play hard to get?" She sits back, crosses her legs, and tries to look coy. Its sexy as hell. I rethink my previous declaration.

12

My dick wants a vote. I deny him.

"Not too hard to get." I smile and take her hand. Her nails are painted blue. Everything about this girl is not my style. Cookie looks like the women I chase. Hair and boobs can only go so far. Blue nails are unpredictable.

"I get a feeling there's more to you than a pretty face."

That's definitely a man's line. She runs her hand down my cheek.

I twist a strand of purple locks around my finger.

"I guarantee there's more to you than purple hair."

I sound like a tweeb.

We sit in a silent checkmate a few seconds, contemplating our next moves. If she wants more, I'll give it to her. I'll give it to her so good.

Of course she wants more. Look at you.

She fingers graze the center of my palm like she's searching for something.

You know what she's looking for.

I lick my lips to satiate the desire to kiss her. This isn't a hook up, if it were, she'd be riding me by now. I want to take things slow.

"What are you thinking right now?" I beat her to the punch.

A shy smile spreads across her face. She shrugs.

"What's that?" I mimic her.

She contemplates so long I start to worry. I want to hit backspace on the keyboard until the question vanishes from the script.

"Aside from you being male," she starts. Her eyes remain on my palm, like she's reading my future. "You aren't the kind of person I would normally go for."

"Why not?" I'm everyone's type, male or female.

"Well, look at you." She gestures. "You're gorgeous and I'm..."

"Beautiful."

She glances up with her bullshit meter on full strength and I'm passing with flying colors. For once in my life I'm not playing a game. This is me, sitting beside a girl with no other intention than getting to know her.

"We come from different places." She doesn't need to elaborate, I get it. I'm wearing expensive kicks and jeans. She's as grunge as they come.

"I look good in flannel." Not that I own any.

"It isn't just the clothes. You're in college and I'm..."

My phone vibrates on the arm of the couch. I flip it over.

"The dude with the fake ID is here. He can wait."

I turn my attention back to her but the moment has passed, she's ready to bail.

"My car is in the lot on the corner." She stands. "I can only afford two hours. I should go."

I'm not ready for this conversation to end. I want to ask her to wait for me but I don't want to look desperate, or clingy, or any other adjective I would use to describe a woman in my situation.

"Let's run into each other again," she suggests.

"I'll be here tomorrow." I reply quick, too eager. Fuck cool points. She needs to know I want her.

"It's Black Wednesday. Everyone will be here."

The night before Thanksgiving is the biggest party night of the year.

"Is that a yes?" I play it off like I'm cool, but inside I'm desperate.

"Does ten work for you?" She fidgets with her phone.

"Ten is good."

We begin walking back to the stairs. She takes my hand, her fingers thread between mine. I stop walking, and spin her around. I press against her, holding one hand behind her back. I turn the sexy up to ten.

"Make it nine." My tone is deep, demanding.

"I'll be here." Her breath tickles my neck when she speaks. She smells like nutmeg or cloves. Spicy and exotic.

She presses her free hand flat against my chest. My heart beats harder in reply like it wants her to reach in and grab hold. I've never been a sentimental person. This girl has me feeling like an Ed Sheeran song.

"Have you ever met a person and felt instant good vibes?"

"Not really," I tease. Levity helps me maintain some shred of manhood. Who am I kidding? I'd let her shred my manhood to pieces.

"Wow. That could've been a moment."

"We can't really have a moment. I don't even know your name." She pulls back and extends her hand.

"Hi. I'm Leeyan."

I bring it to my lips knowing this will be the only kiss I give her tonight.

"Nice to meet you. I'm Giovanni."

CHAPTER ONE

Now

Guys like me have an expiration date. Unlike actors or musicians, male entertainers don't get better with age. It isn't the brutal fitness program or never-ending meal prep that force us off the stage. There is only one thing powerful enough to make a guy hang up his G-strings for a nine to five job.

A woman.

Not just any chick with a trust fund and a nice ass. It takes a special kind of female. The one who shaves your back before a show and stays up late with a bottle of champagne waiting for you to come home after a long night in the club. A woman who does kinky shit to your dick you've only seen on dark-web porn.

The kind of woman who ruins you.

When the novelty of dating a stripper wears off, the accusations begin. You're cheating or want to cheat, or about to cheat. She's tired of defending your profession to her tribe. She's over feeling self-conscious when you come home smelling like another woman's perfume. By the time this happens the dude is so pussy-whipped he convinces himself, he can't live without her.

Then it's bye-bye Trance, hello Target.

I've seen it a dozen times over the six years I've been at the club. Some of the best dancers I know are working shit jobs at Costco and Home Depot because some woman came along with a magical vagina.

A few tried to come back, but it's never the same. Women can smell desperation and isn't a turn on. Just like in baseball, when you're out, you're out.

Trance is my day job. Steady, taxable income. My side game is where I make real money. It's also where the freaky shit happens. That's part of the fun. You never know what's waiting on the other side of the door. Some jobs are run of the mill sex for cash, but there are times when I have no idea what to expect. Unlike my clients who have researched online, watched videos of me on stage. They know exactly what they're getting. The only thing I can count on is the stack of green waiting for me at the end of the date. The Beatles had it all wrong–money is all you need.

I turn into the garage beneath my building and park in my usual spot. The space costs an extra five hundred a month; my fully-loaded Audi A5 is worth it. It's going to hurt like hell when my lease is up and I give her back to the dealership. As much as I love her, I'm not ready to make her mine. Buying a car is a huge commitment.

Nothing in my life is permanent. Even when I thought I had a plan, the universe was plotting against me. One day I'm playing college baseball with my best friend, six months later he's a dad, and I'm taking my clothes off for money.

I lock the car and take the stairs to the main floor. Fred catches me in the monitors and spins around. He's not quite a doorman, but I wouldn't call him a security guard either. His job is to sit at the main entrance and watch the security cameras. He mostly just watches Netflix.

"Early night." He checks his watch. Fred knows I work at the club—he's prevented more than one stalker from pulling a fifty shades of crazy on me.

"Slow night." I stop and pound his fist. "Anything exciting happening around here?" I walk to the mailboxes on the wall opposite Fred's post.

Most of the units in this building are empty. With a housing shortage in the city, that may seem odd, but the owner of the building makes more money renting them on Airbnb.

"Dickhead on the tenth floor is back for the weekend, and there are two overnighters on three."

I pause for dramatic effect. "Male or female?"

"Couldn't tell." He spins back. "But they look like your type."

I scoff and pull a stack of junk mail out of my box. "Have a good one, Fred."

"You too, youngblood."

The concrete floors and gray furniture in my apartment give off a chilly vibe. I call it modern, my best friend Theo calls it cold. His place is warm. Too warm for me with all those bodies hanging around. He isn't even banging his babysitter anymore, but she's always there with her son, warming up the place.

I drop my bag next to the door and kick off my Nikes. Each movement echoes into the empty room. I tap the switch on the wall to turn on the light as I undress on my way to the bathroom. It's ridiculous that I'm showering before a Skype; Antonia wouldn't even mind—she's kinky that way. One night she instructed me not to shower before meeting for our date. I spent three hours at the gym that morning, and by the time I met up with her, I could barely stand the smell. We ended up in her hot tub, but everything that happened before I stepped into the chlorinated water was raw and dirty.

After my shower, I sit at my desk, shirtless, wearing nothing but a pair of loose shorts. I have a semi; I always get wood when I see her. Antonia is the closest thing I've ever had to a relationship, except she pays me for sex. Still, we spent holidays and birthdays together. She even hooked me up with this apartment. Antonia Zar inherited her family's international real estate company. She has access to the most powerful and influential people in the world, and when we're together, she makes me feel like one of them. She has her hand in a lot of pots—fashion, tequila, real estate, even yachts.

We met at her fall show. She was impressed with my walk, and my cock. Nine months later, she offered me a job running her nightclub in Rio. Club Silk is on the outskirts of the red-light district and always under scrutiny by the local police, mainly because the locals she hires to run the club are easily swayed by gangsters and pimps. Antonia thinks having an American running the club will draw more tourists. American clubs in Brazil attract rich kids looking to party without getting robbed.

Right from the beginning, Antonia made it clear that she doesn't give free rides. Neither do I. If I want to be taken seriously by Antonia's staff and business associates,

I can't be her boy toy, which is why I insisted on paying my way to Rio. I trust Antonia, but I have to be able to support myself in case shit goes south.

I was ready to pack up and move to Brazil the morning after she offered me the job, but Antonia wouldn't let me. She said I have to be free of strings here before I go, being tied to the past prevents you from moving forward. I rarely see my parents; they aren't holding me here. My best friend is too busy playing daddy to be my wingman, and if I'm not working or in the gym, I'm home alone. It's a strange feeling when you wake up one day and realize you aren't anyone's number one. I'm always surrounded by people, but none of them know me. They see my face, my body, the parts of me I sell. I don't even know who I am most days.

My phone buzzes on the desk. It's a text from Theo thanking me for hooking him up with the job at Trance. It isn't a done deal—I still have to talk to Jim—but I've spent six months working out with Theo, getting him stage ready. I text back the middle finger emoji, a term of endearment with us. Theo is one of the few people in my life I give a shit about. When he's happy, I'm happy. When he's fucked up, it fucks me up. His ex fucked him up, which in turn fucked me up.

It was my decision to leave school. I've never been good at learning, and Theo was the only reason I applied to college. Once he left to play daddy, there was no reason for me to stay. Baseball wasn't my dream. I probably would've quit playing ball in high school if it wasn't for Theo. He pitched, I played catcher, and I hated every second of it. I wanted to be in the outfield, not crouched behind home plate, but I made Theo a better pitcher. I suffered for him, because that's what friends do.

After I left school, I tried to find what my father considers "real" work—construction, painting, plumbing—but I'm not a blue-collar guy. I'm not my dad. It kills him to know his son can't plunge a toilet. Hell, I don't even own a plunger. His expectations of me are unreasonable. I can't fix a toilet or change my own tire, so what. It doesn't make me less of a man. I know this. My father does not agree.

My computer starts to ring. I accept the call and Antonia appears on the screen. Her long black hair is gathered over one shoulder, hiding her only tattoo—a blue dolphin that arches over her heart.

"Gio!" she exclaims in a way only foreign women can pull off.

"Hello, beautiful." My voice is an octave lower than normal so I don't sound like a teenage boy coming through her speakers.

"How's Paris?"

"Cold," she pouts. "How is my favorite city in the world?"

"Cold."

"Then let's talk about someplace warm. How soon can you be in Rio?"

"Uh, can I get back to you on that?"

"My manager—that whore—is pregnant and decided my club is no place for a mother to be working."

She throws her hands in the air and begins to babble I have no idea what she's saying or if she's even speaking English.

"I need you, Gio. If you can't come soon, I'll have to get someone else..."

"I'll be there. I just need a few months to wrap things up."

She looks directly into the camera. "This is the big time, darling. My club pulls in three, four hundred a night—a *night*, Gio." Her accent makes everything she says overly dramatic. "You can't tell me yes today then change your mind in a month. I can pull someone from my club in Monaco."

Her threats are empty, but the last thing I want to do is piss her off. Truth be told, I want this job in Brazil more than anything.

"Give me three months." I have enough money to go now, but I want more than enough. "I'll be there by fall."

Money isn't the only thing holding me back. I have to get a work permit and visa.

"Bravo! That's the fire I want to see under your gorgeous ass. Now stand up and turn around."

I laugh and lean back in my chair.

"I'm serious, Gio. I need to see my favorite ass in the world." She motions with her finger for me to get up and twirl.

So much for being treated with respect.

CHAPTER TWO

I'm always on edge before dinner with my parents. A shot of whiskey is mandatory before breaking bread with my father. Dropping out of college, quitting baseball, and then working at Trance—it's a trifecta of disappointment. My dad, Alberto Castillo, is a standup guy, a hard worker, and a bunch of other qualities I lack. His idea of happiness is a roof over his head and food in the cabinets. Anything else is a waste of his hard-earned money. When I wanted a new pair of Jordans or even just a new tire for my bike, it came with a lecture on laziness or entitlement. Dad always believed I was an ungrateful kid. He would sit in his chair and glower at me every time I reached for seconds at dinner, like I was stealing his food. He's the kind of man who demanded respect while everyone else had to earn it.

After I quit baseball, the minuscule amount of pride my father had for me vanished. There is nothing I can do to win it back, and working as a male dancer certainly doesn't help my cause. Dad would rather have me cleaning toilets with him—you know, "honest" work. At the end of the day, he's still a janitor, and I'm still a whore.

He won't even look out the window to see my car, because in his mind I didn't earn it, because I'm not a real man—real men don't take their clothes off for money.

I plan on telling my parents about Brazil tonight. The sooner the better. Telling them puts me on the hook. Any reservations I have about moving will diminish once I'm forced to defend my decision to my father.

The phone near my front door rings. It's a direct line to Fred.

"What's up?" I answer.

"Your Uber is here."

Since I plan to drink copious amounts of wine at dinner, I ordered an Uber.

"Be right down."

Fred has to announce all my visitors, it's part of the job and one reason the rent in this building is so high. I pay a fraction of what my neighbors pay. Antonia claims to have pulled some strings to get me into this building. I think she owns it. She won't admit it and I don't ask. Knowing only proves my father right. I didn't earn this address, it was given to me.

The Uber driver is quiet, probably mid-thirties, definitely foreign. I wonder if he left his family to pick me up. It's Sunday evening and he's still out driving people around the city.

No days off, even for Uber drivers.

On the rare occasion I drive, my father makes it a personal conquest to make me feel like a traitor to my country for driving a German car. He's second-generation Italian-American. After a few glasses of wine, you'd think he just stepped off the boat. My mother was born in Palermo, and sometimes I think dad is jealous of her authenticity.

"Have a nice night," the driver says as he stops in front of my parents' house. I tip him ten dollars cash.

Unlike most California coastal communities, the Avenues are blanketed with fog and covered in a salty mist. Everything rusts. Thanks to the damp, everything molds, too. Even the sidewalk is peppered with patches of moss seeping out of the concrete.

Cars line every inch of the street; there are more vehicles than houses. I walk between a Mini Cooper and a Volvo to get to the sidewalk, and that's when I notice a FOR SALE sign staked into the dirt under my tree. I say my tree because I planted it when I was four. The city went through a beautification process and decided to plant trees and greenery in our neighborhood. They involved the residents by allowing them to take ownership of the newly planted vegetation in front of their homes. Mom chose a tree. I named him Tree.

I open the front door and time-travel back to my childhood—the smell of meatballs frying, the cloud of smoke wafting from the front room where my father is watching television. Mom yells from the kitchen.

"Giovanni is that you?" Mom came to America when she was six, and her parents moved back to Italy after they retired. If she had her way, she'd join them.

I unravel my Burberry scarf and hang it on a hook in the hall, followed by my coat. Mom's shoes clack against the hardwood as she walks out to greet me.

"*Patanino!*" She still calls me her 'little potato' even though I'm over six feet tall. I'll always be her baby; that's how moms are—some moms.

"Hey Ma."

She grabs my head and pulls me down to her level so she can kiss my cheeks. "I made your favorite." She releases me and walks back to the kitchen with a towel slung over her right shoulder. "I don't want to hear no baloney about not eating carbs. Nobody ever died from eating carbs."

"Yes, Ma." I only visit my parents once a month, and during these visits I eat carbs—lots of them.

Dad doesn't greet me. He sits in his worn-out leather recliner wearing his red plaid pajama pants and wool socks. I can barely make out the faded Local 248 logo on his t-shirt. His Sunday clothes, he calls them.

"Alberto!" Mom yells from the kitchen. "Get the wine."

Dad grumbles, lowers the level on his chair. It bangs and launches forward. He finally acknowledges me. "You drink white?"

It's more of an accusation than a question. He knows I prefer white but he asks anyway. "White works for me."

He huffs and walks toward the liquor cabinet. "I can't have a son who drinks red, like a real man."

Today its wine, last month my car—tomorrow he'll find some other reason to hate me.

"Red is fine too, Dad."

Dad returns from the kitchen with two bottles of wine and sets them on the dining table nestled into the opposite corner of the room. My parents' house is butted up to the neighbors on both sides, and the only natural light comes from the window behind the TV. The old lamp my grandparents gave us when I was ten. It gives off a dim orange glow making everyone and everything look sickly.

He opens the white first and pours me a glass. "You hungry?"

To prepare for tonight's carb fest, I fasted twelve hours and ran fifteen miles on the treadmill this morning.

"I could eat." I sit in my seat.

Mom walks in and sets a platter of spaghetti and meat sauce on the table. I pour her a glass of white wine then top off my glass. Dad broods across the table with his red. I wait until he's served himself before putting a single thing on my plate.

"How's work?" Mom always leads the dinner conversation.

I slurp a forkful of spaghetti and barely chew before swallowing. It's hard to enjoy the first few bites because I'm wolfing it down.

"Oh, so he works now." Dad takes a dig at me while my mouth is full.

Nothing's changed. My parents talk about me like I'm not here or I'm too dense to follow the conversation. I'm actually too hungry to interject.

"You should be proud of Gio," she chastises. "He makes money for himself." Mom winks at me. "And he's a good boy."

Mom's idea of a good boy is one who didn't knock up a girl out of wedlock. She likes Theo, but let's face it, he's a sinner.

Dad grumbles and rips a piece of bread from the loaf. He dips it in the sauce before folding it into his mouth. "How does he make all this money? He doesn't have a real job." Even with a mouthful of bread, the hits keep coming.

I set down my fork and pound my wine. It's time to defend myself.

"I'm working for a furniture company part-time, and I'm still doing the modeling." Half-truths.

"Modeling!" Dad slams his fist on the table, sending his fork jumping off his plate. "Men don't model."

"Some men do." Mom looks to me as if I should name a man my father would respect.

I go blank.

"De Niro," she blurts out. "He modeled suits—I saw it in Vogue magazine." Mom spins her pasta against a spoon with a proud expression.

"Bullshit." Dad stabs at a meatball. "And even if he did, he's Robert fucking De Niro."

I give my mom a *don't bother* look. There's nothing she can say to make him think better of me.

When I'm here, it feels like I never left. I'm a kid again, trying to please my father, eating everything Mom puts on my plate.

I move to a safe topic. It's not one my mother or I will enjoy, but it's safe.

"How's work, Dad?"

Dad launches into his latest grievances about the dipshit of the month. Al's been working maintenance since before I was born, and it's a good job as far as pay and benefits. Maintenance supervisor is the official title, but that doesn't make what he does respectable—not to me.

It wasn't like Dad worked hard to provide a better life for us. He never bought property or invested. Thanks to rent control and a landlord who inherited the property from her parents, my family has been able to stay in this house for twenty-seven years. I can't imagine them being anywhere else. They would never dream of leaving.

"Maybe it's time to retire." Mom dabs her mouth with a napkin. "We don't know what Josie will do." She shrugs and looks at Dad. They've been married almost thirty years. A single look from my mom and he knows exactly what she's thinking.

In some ways, their relationship is a beautiful thing. In others, it's a nightmare. To be with one person for that long seems impossible. Maybe thirty years ago falling in love and getting married at twenty-years-old was normal. That was before Tinder.

"I don't wanna talk about it right now." Dad jerks his head in my direction.

"What's going on with Josie? Are they selling the house next door?" I remember the sign out front. The same family owns three houses on this block.

"Mr. Granger died," Dad says. "He was old."

I drink from my wine glass and add up the years in my head. "He must have been pushing one hundred."

"Ninety-seven," Mom confirms.

Dad remarks about how Josie's been waiting for him to die. I kind of agree. The only way to get an old person out of a house in San Francisco is death or an owner move-in. Lucky for us, Josie doesn't need the money. She has property all over the city and is married to a doctor.

"How old are Josie's kids now?" She always had a kid in a stroller and one cooking in the oven.

"Her youngest is graduating high school next month." Mom starts to fidget. She gives the pasta in the center of the table a quick toss then motions for me to lift my plate. I do as I'm told and let her pile on a disturbing amount of spaghetti. "Erin finished college this year, and she's in fashion." She gives me that classic mom look.

"No. Please don't even say it."

"Erin?" Dad wonders. "That's the one with the lazy eye?"

I laugh and a meatball almost shoots out of my mouth. "Yeah, that's the one."

"Can you imagine what your kids will look like?" Dad makes a really inappropriate face.

"Stop it!" Mom yells. "Shame on you both." She walks to the kitchen with her plate, and a few seconds later the sink turns on.

"Sorry, Ma," I yell to her.

Dad waves for me to stop apologizing. "She knows."

The simplicity in his reply makes me smile. My parents don't always agree or like each other, but who needs like when you have love?

Dad lowers his tone and leans in toward me. "You saw the sign?"

I put down my fork and reach for the bread. "Yeah, is it for next door?"

Dad pushes the loaf toward me and taps his finger on the table.

I give him a confused look. "What do you mean?"

"Here."

"Here?"

"Yes, here."

I finally catch on. "Josie is selling this house!"

Mom drops a plate into the sink.

"Keep your voice down!" Dad sits up and sips his wine. "She doesn't want to talk about it with you."

Mom doesn't like to worry people. She worries enough for everyone.

"She offered the house to us at 'a *good price*'." He scoffs and shakes his head as if it wasn't low enough.

My father isn't balking at the price because the house isn't worth it; he just can't afford it. The city grew around him like my tree. He stayed here, rooted into the cement, unwilling or unable to leave—pun intended. Now he can't afford to buy the house or move into a new one. He's stuck.

"Maybe you can get a loan. You have decent credit, don't you?" I assume my parents have credit and savings. Those are things adults should have. "This place isn't in the best shape. You can negotiate."

"Not in this market."

This is San Francisco, top of the food chain—people buy shacks for half a million dollars. This house is an untouched gold mine. A young tech family would kill to have it. It's like a blank canvas waiting to become a hipster's paradise.

"What's going to happen when the place sells?"

"It's up to the new owners."

I imagine the moral dilemma I will face if my parents have to move. Would I invite them to stay with me? Would they want to?

Dad goes back to his food. "This isn't your problem."

"But I grew up here..." I start to get sentimental.

"This isn't your house," Dad reminds me. I detect a double meaning.

I couldn't wait to get out from under *his* roof, but all of my childhood memories remain within these walls. I look at the corner where our Christmas tree stands every year. Mom has a bookshelf there now, but it gets moved right after Thanksgiving to make way for the fake tree we've had since I was eleven. The chair I'm sitting in has been *my* chair ever since I can remember. I've blown out all of my birthday candles from this seat.

"Did you see the Giant's new first baseman? He's Brazilian."

I choke on a noodle. "Brazilian, really?"

While Dad prattles on about batting averages, I realize I'm not even going to be here for Christmas this year. It knocks me back a step. I decide not to tell them about Brazil until I'm further along in the process. I'm not saying my parents losing their home is a game-changer, but it is a new level. One I never thought I'd have to face.

Two hours and three thousand carbs later, I leave my parents' house second-guessing my life. I spend the better part of the night thinking about Brazil—or more like stressing about Brazil. I wonder what my father will say when I tell him I'm leaving. Mom will cry; that's a given. How will Dad feel? Just another notch on the wall of shame.

Well, the shame goes both ways.

My parents shouldn't even be renting at their age. By my father's standards, the men at Trace are lowlife pieces of shit, hustlers, and whores, but half of those whores own property. What does Alberto Castillo own? Nothing.

I'd rather die in a favela in Rio, than end up like my father.

CHAPTER THREE

I spend more time role playing for clients than living my own life. For a thousand dollars, I'll dress like your ex-husband and let you spank me. I'll prepare a five-star meal in my underwear or clean your house naked. I'm all about the needs and wants of my clientele.

Today, I'm the Christian Grey of Trance.

It takes balls to step on stage and command attention from a room of inebriated, self-entitled women. Playing a cocky billionaire makes it slightly easier. The men of Trance are expected to be hairless, hard, and hot as fuck. If you falter in one of those areas, you can always try bartending. Trance only hires the best of the best, and I don't eat bland chicken and steamed broccoli five nights a week because I love food that tastes like cardboard. Zero body fat is required of male dancers.

A little jiggle in the right place can be sexy on a woman. A half-decent looking female dancer with average tits will always get a few dollars tossed her way, but it's a different game for men. If you can't bounce a quarter off your abs, don't bother taking the stage.

Trance is set up to look like a high-end lounge, like something you'd see at the top of a five-star hotel. Men don't need fancy booths and crystal stemware. Give them a chair and a naked chick spinning on a pole, and they're cool. Women, though—they want the illusion, the fantasy. The what-ifs, wishes, and shoulda-coulda-wouldas keep Trance's doors open. I take it a step further. For the right price, I'll turn a what-if into what's next.

"Hey, Gio, wait up."

I turn and see Percy. He's one of the house duds. They clean up after us and serve drinks; it's part of the process. It's how you pay your dues.

I pause with my hand on the locker room door. "What?"

"Just checking to see if we're on for next week."

Percy is honest and works hard, but his ambition is a red flag—I don't trust anyone who balls as hard as me. After harassing Rico for weeks, he finally booked Percy on a side job, with me.

"Rico's the boss. He handles all the details." I turn to go inside.

"I know, I just thought you might want to run through the game plan with me beforehand."

Fucking hell.

"I like to wing it." I slap his back and leave him in the hall, where he belongs.

The locker room at Trance is a stark contrast to the main room. It's dark, dirty, and smells like ball sweat. Home sweet home.

I bust through the door. "Looks like rain, boys!"

Rico pumps his fist in response. He runs the side game. His company, The Agency, books private events ranging from your standard bachelorette parties to dinner parties with the Zuckerbergs. The guy who booked that gig works directly for Mark now.

Opportunity is everywhere.

Rico is waiting at my locker. "It's always jumpin' on a warm night."

He's right—something about nice weather brings the women out like cats in heat.

"The line is halfway down the street." I fist-bump Rico.

He lowers his voice and looks over his shoulder at Thor and Dain. They're deep into their pre-show rituals.

"I have a money job for you." Money job is code for sex. "Are you *up* for it?" he jokes.

"Always. Text me the info."

Unlike the other guys, I have no moral qualms about fucking for money. Thor limits his side work to bridal showers and birthday parties, while Dain's moral compass depends on the direction of the wind. He looks and acts more like a cop than a stripper, which is probably why women love him. He takes care of his nephew and his brother's ex, and being someone his family can be proud of is vital to Dain. I've given up trying to impress my father. To him, I'm a lost cause. The feeling is mutual.

Jim strolls into the locker room with a cigar hanging from the corner of his mouth. I can always smell when he's nearby. Rumor has is it he was connected to an Irish gang on the east coast in his younger days. He moved to the Bay Area to start over in the nineties, and bought this dilapidated building before the dot.com boom. Before it was Trance, this place was a titty bar, an Irish pub, and a teahouse. The teahouse was a front for a Chinese gambling ring.

"Evening, gents."

We greet Jim with the usual grumble of hellos and fuck-offs.

"Good news, boys—its lady's choice." He delivers the announcement with a throaty laugh, and the guys toss a mouthful of complaints at him. They bounce off Jim with a flick of his cigar.

Ladies choice was a marketing gimmick created to get more followers on social media. To our dismay, it worked. Jim sets up a poll on Facebook where people get to vote on songs. Doesn't seem like a big deal, but you haven't seen the song list.

"Quit your fuckin' bellyaching." Jim holds out his black and gray hooligan hat filled with torn strips of paper.

Thor picks first. "'All About That Bass'?" He looks up in confusion. "It's a song about fish?"

"It's bass, fucktard, not bass," Rico interjects, enlightening him.

"Oh yeah, I know that song." Thor nods. "It's poppy."

Thor's just over thirty, which is old for our industry. His knowledge of music and pop culture in general is limited. Thor likes to read, and he's always got his nose stuck in a book. When he's not reading, he's working out. His body is a temple, and women love to worship it. He isn't much of a dancer, but he's a master of the sore neck— his signature move. He tilts his head to the ceiling, grabs the back of his neck, and rotates his hips in slow circular movements. Then he lowers his head with an expression he calls "painful pleasure". When I do the sore neck, I imagine the way it feels when I'm getting a shitty blow job, that out-of-control sensation when a woman is sucking you off then accidentally scrapes your dick with her teeth.

Rico pulls his song. "Yes," he hisses. "'Dark Horse'."

Fuck. He got the golden ticket. Jim always throws in one good song, and Katy Perry's "Dark Horse" has a killer bass drop.

Jim shoves the hat in my direction. I finger the strips, hoping luck is on my side. I finally pull one and unfold it.

Fuck me.

Dain picks the last strip from the hat. "'Take It Off.'"

"I'll trade you," I offer. "I can work with Kesha."

Dain looks at my paper. "'Milkshake'?"

Rico starts singing the lyrics. "*My milkshake brings all the boys to yard...*" He does a little ass shake and Thor whips him with his towel.

"Fuck that." Dain retreats to his locker.

"Come on, Dain," I plead. "I can't do my routine to this. It's a boner-killer. I'll pay you."

Dain looks back like he's interested. "How much?"

"A bill."

"Fuck off. At least two bills."

"One and I'll give you dibs on my song next month."

"One bill, dibs on your song next month, and a bottle of that spray you gave me for Christmas last year."

"Fuck that." I walk away.

The spray he's talking about was Armani.

"Nice not doing business with you." Dain drops his pants and wraps a towel around his waist. "Have fun shaking your milk," he yells as he walks to the shower.

"Come on, Jim. Have mercy." I hand him back my slip. "They're gonna laugh me off the stage."

Giggling is okay, but straight laughing at your performance will destroy your ego.

39

"The point of ladies' night is mixing shit up." He points at my strip of paper. "That song was the most requested this week."

"Gee, thanks."

Jim opens the door and yells for Damon, another dud. Three seconds later, a younger, better-looking version of Will Smith appears at the door.

"This place is a fucking pigsty." He motions for Damon to enter. "Get some clean towels, sweep, and bleach the fucking toilets." Jim ticks off each task on his fingers.

"I'm on it." Damon goes straight to work gathering the dirty towels we lazily tossed on the floor.

Jim puts these guys through the ringer. If they keep showing up at a shit job for shit pay, it proves they'll be reliable when they're called up to the stage. Work ethic is everything when it comes to dancing.

"Jim, can I get a minute?" I ask before he walks into the hall. He motions for me to follow him. I pull on a white t-shirt and we walk through the maze of hallways to his office. We call it the green mile, like that Tom Hanks movie where they walk prisoners down a green walkway to the electric chair. If you find yourself walking these halls, you're on the wrong side of doing what's right.

Jim sits at his sizeable brown desk, which takes up most of the room. The stench of stale cigars and dirty carpet makes the space almost intolerable.

"What can I do for you, kid?"

"Have you given any thought to bringing on another dancer?"

It's been a few months since I pitched the idea of hiring Theo.

Jim makes a grunting sound. "You know how the system works, Gio." His chair groans beneath him as he leans back. "Damon is next up, and he's a good kid. He's paid his dues."

"I know, but Theo can dance. There wouldn't be any learning curve—he can jump right into the routines." My argument is weak.

"We have a system," Jim repeats. "I've got two duds waiting in the wings. How would it look if we brought in fresh meat?"

"We can say Theo is from another club. Say you poached him from Vegas or LA."

Jim gives a slow nod as he opens the wooden box on his desk and pulls out a fresh cigar. He's contemplating my proposal as he goes through the process of cutting and lighting it. He inhales and the tip glows red. Smoke billows into the room.

"I don't know, kid. Damon is a good dancer too, and he's got that Caribbean act going for him. He can be a gold mine."

Jim's right. Damon does a killer accent. If he hadn't told us he grew up in East Oakland, I'd swear he just walked off a beach in Aruba.

I have one more card to play.

"I won't take my finder's fee, and I know Theo is going to be a money maker." A finder's fee at Trance is twenty percent, and Jim would have to pay me a cut of whatever Theo makes for the house.

Places like Trance are always looking for fresh talent because the turnover rate in our industry is high. Women, drugs, shame—the list of reasons why people leave is not as long as the reasons they find themselves at the back door looking for a job. Theo literally picks up dog shit for a living. He can barely afford food. He is willing to do whatever it takes to make sure Lulu has the best life has to offer.

"He's a real dancer?" Jim raises an eyebrow and gives me a half-smile.

I've got him interested.

"Been taking classes since we were kids."

"And he's ready now?"

"Just a few afternoons with Ivy and he'll blow Rico and Dain out of the water." None of us are real dancers, not like Theo. Ivy's choreography is simple enough for us to look like we know what we're doing, but Theo's going to kill it.

Jim sighs and leans back in his chair. "All right, I'll call her tomorrow and see when she can fit him in. If she doesn't think he's stage ready, all bets are off and I move Damon up."

"You won't be disappointed." I stand and open the door. "You have a heart of gold, Jim."

"Wait, kid." Jim stands. "Noticed you've been taking a lot of side jobs with Rico."

"It's the grind." I flash him my bullshit smile. "I've got dreams, Jimbo." Jim is the last person I'm going to tell about Brazil, mainly because he's going to blow a gasket, then try to talk me out of leaving.

"Be smart, kid." Jim is concerned, but he won't speak out of turn. I'm a grown man; I don't need anyone telling me how to live my life. I like that about Jim—he can be concerned without judgment.

I get more than enough judgment from my father.

We start the main show with a group performance. Ironically, this month is baseball themed. We start off in uniforms: a jersey and tight baseball pants with a little extra padding in the crotch area—not that I need it, but the bigger the bulge, the better the tips. By the end of the two-minute routine, we're shirtless, baseball hats on backward, bats at the ready position. Just when the ladies are nice and hot, the train wreck begins.

Thor takes the stage to Megan Trainor's "All About That Bass". We don't watch each other's routines, especially on ladies' nights. When Thor doesn't return to the locker room after his solo, it's a good sign. Thor's fuck spot is the utility closet. He keeps a stash of condoms and wet wipes on a shelf for nights like this.

"You're up, Gio." Jimbo gives me the two-minute warning.

I grab my pump and head to the bathroom. Women tip more when they think you're packing serious meat. I rub a little lube over my limp dick and place it into the clear tube. My pump has a trigger handle, like the kind you see on a garden hose. I pump it and watch the gauge as I build suction. When I feel my cock inflate, I slowly release the trigger, and the tube starts to lose pressure. I let it go for a few seconds then press the trigger again. I wouldn't say it feels good, not like the suction of a woman's mouth, but it does the job. I slip out of the pump with a dick full of blood and tie off. This hard-on is good for at least fifteen minutes, and that's all I need for my solo. I tuck my swollen cock into my slacks and head to the main room.

Rico is waiting for me just outside the dressing room. He is over six feet tall and built like a linebacker, but the motherfucker is stealthy as hell.

"God damn, Rico." I jump back. "Why are you always hidin' in the shadows?"

"All my best work is done in the dark, son." He slaps my back. "I got an early private."

Private dances go for two hundred and fifty to five hundred dollars, and time is sold in fifteen-minute increments. Privates are where the money is.

"This is the fourth time she's booked me. I think she's ready to go to the next level." Next level means a private meeting outside the club. Poaching clients from Trance is a big no-no, but that doesn't stop Rico, or me, from doing it.

I stop at the door to the main room, stage right. I focus on the darkness in front of me and get into character.

Arrogant, entitled, rich.

Rico pretends to straighten my collar. I swat his hand away.

He pats my shoulder and says, "Go get that paper."

I nod and toss him a sideways glance. "Easy money," I boast.

Rico leaves just as my music drops.

It's my song, not the ladies' choice. Jim will give me a verbal beating, but I'd rather be called a cock-sucking pussy boy than face the humiliation of trying to play Christian Grey to "Milkshake". The choice was easy. I just thought, *what would Mr. Grey do?* After our group routine, I paid a visit to the DJ booth and slipped Andre fifty bucks to forget it's ladies night.

I take the stage wearing a black suit, gray tie, and crisp white shirt. A dim spotlight follows me around, and the screen behind me projects a replica image of the red room from the movie. A large bed flashes on the screen, and I set a chair in front of it.

Some guys let Jim pick a woman from the audience, a bride-to-be or birthday girl. They're usually fun and roll deep with friends willing to pay for their humiliation. I don't go for the obvious victim, though. I like a challenge. Women who sit on stage covering their faces are useless to me. I get rid of them quick, and I'm not even nice about it—I don't have to be, since I'm playing a sadist.

Real money isn't made on the stage. I'm in it for the extra, the one-on-one sessions. Birthday girls rarely go for a private dance—too much judgment from their friends. I'm looking for a particular type of woman, one who's confident and reeks of money.

It doesn't take long to spot her.

She isn't jumping in the air for attention or hiding behind a co-worker. My submissive is daring me to choose her with a smug I'm-too-good-for-you stare.

I walk down the stairs stage left through a throng of arms and hands that grab at my suit like I'm a rock star. Being desired is a rush, but the feeling is temporary, like a line of blow or an orgasm. The harder the challenge, the better the rush.

She tosses back the rest of her martini and whispers to her friend to watch her purse. By the time I offer my hand, she's on her feet and ready to go.

I walk her back to the chair on stage. The lights go from dim yellow to red, and the crowd loses their shit. The room is electrified and I'm standing in a puddle of water. If I fail to entertain the mob to their expectations, my career is over.

Fuck the five-star reviews.

Fuck the video montage of my best performances.

Fuck me if I don't get this right.

I wonder if Beyoncé feels this way before a concert.

The chorus drops, and I fall to my knees. I lean in and pretend to kiss her neck as I pump between her legs.

"What's your name, beautiful?" I run my lips across her throat and feel her swallow.

"Shelly."

I would've guessed something cuter, like Camille or Porsche. With her blonde hair, hazelnut eyes, and creamy skin, she doesn't look like a Shelly.

"I'm Giovanni."

"I know. I drove all the way from Stockton to see you tonight."

A fan—nice.

"Thank you for coming." I let the inside of my lips brush her earlobe.

Shelly's eyes roll back, and she grips my forearms.

Too easy.

I stand up and back away so she can recover.

I tease the ladies sitting in the front row with a few hip rolls as I unbutton my shirt. Then I pull the tie from my neck, wrapping it around my hand as I walk back to Shelly. I kneel in front of her and press my mouth to her inner thigh. She inches her ass to the edge of the chair, closer to my face.

Too eager.

I wrap the tie around her wrist and pull her arms behind her back, securing her hands to the chair. The song changes to the one that played in the movie the first time Grey fucks Anna in the playroom. As the crowd cheers, I step off stage for a quick outfit change.

Percy is waiting for me. I step out of the slacks and pull on a pair of three-hundred-dollar jeans, ripped and distressed to perfection. Percy doesn't say a word; hell, he won't even make eye contact. I'm in the zone. Christian Grey ain't got nothing on me.

I return to the stage shirtless and shoeless with an arrogant, animalistic scowl. I grab a champagne bottle filled with water placed stage right then stand in front of Shelly and pour water down my chest. It's warm so the chill doesn't cause my balls to shrivel up.

I sit on Shelly's lap and pump my fake boner into her stomach. Her back arches, lifting her breasts toward my face. These little signs let me know she's down for anything. I nestle my face in her cleavage.

She bites her lip and smiles.

We're so on book right now, my balls tingle. I'm confident Shelly wants to fuck me, but I'm not Thor. I won't drag her to the storage room for a quickie after my routine—I don't fuck for free.

I untie Shelly's hands and help her stand. I quickly bend her over, and she grips the seat of the chair. I raise my hand back and rock her body forward in hard jerky motions to give the illusion that I'm spanking her. I alternate between slapping her ass and pounding her like we're fucking doggy style. The thirty-second light flashes. I spin her around so she's standing in my arms. Just as the music fades, I place a tender kiss on her forehead.

"If you want a private dance, let your server know," I whisper in her ear, pressing my dick into her side.

She nods.

As the stage lights fade to black, I slowly back away.

When a woman leaves the stage after my routine, she feels special, like she turned me on. That is why I book more privates than any of the other entertainers.

Rico is the pretty boy. My body isn't as toned as Dain's or as strong as Thor's, but I can convince a mother of four to spend her grocery money on fifteen minutes with me in a room the size of a linen closet. Like a good cologne, I want to linger in the back of her mind. A month from now, when she's doing the dishes or folding laundry, I want her to think of me.

To want me.

When they can't get you out of their heads, they come back. Return customers are what we strive for; regulars pay the bills.

It's important to keep it all business. Men who succeed in the game know how to keep their feelings in check. Just because a woman shows up every week and drops a few hundred dollars on you doesn't mean she loves you. Hell, she might not even like you. The time you spend together is fantasy, and crossing into her real life turns that fantasy into a nightmare.

When a hot chick comes in to celebrate her twenty-first birthday, she's here for a laugh with her girls, a story to tell, a photo op for Instagram. We're not boyfriend material. It's important to remember Trance is not a singles bar. We're here to put on a show, not find a girlfriend. The cougar with the Black AMEX and private town car doesn't want a relationship. She's here to feel wanted again.

You know what happens when someone like Shelly sees us in the wild? They run because cruising the produce section of Whole Foods with your kids and running into the man who pretended to fuck you doggy style in front of your co-workers can be a little uncomfortable.

Most men, myself included, have let our egos take a hit. Unless you learn to keep your guard up and your pride in check, you'll keep taking those jabs. There is no happily ever after for guys like us. I'm not saying it doesn't happen, but it's rare to find love in the club. Love and egos have no place in Trance. We're here for one thing, and one thing only.

Money.

CHAPTER FOUR

Theo's first night at Trance exceeds Jim's expectations. He corners me before my private dance to tell me so.

"That kid is gold." Jim holds his hand out. I take it, and he gives me a bro hug. "I almost feel bad keeping your finder's fee."

I give him a look like it's not too late.

"Not a chance, pretty boy."

We walk down the green mile towards the locker room, and I consider telling Jim about Brazil. I'm irreplaceable, but Theo is a great addition to the Trance line-up. His success will soften the blow.

"Jim, you got a minute?" I stop shy of the locker room.

"I've got tons." He looks at his watch and pulls the cigar from his mouth. "You have privates booked back-to-back."

"Really?"

"I saw four cards on deck for you."

That's a thousand dollars in my pocket for an hour's worth of work.

"Well, what is it, kid?"

"Nothing." I puss out."We can talk later."

"Then get your ass to the booth!" He ashes his cigar on the floor as he walks away.

I forgo the pump and decide to slather a layer of coconut oil on my arms and chest. Something about smelling like the beach turns women on.

The private rooms are a row of doors, the space inside no bigger than a kitchen pantry. Each room is equipped with a high back chair, the kind you see in a fancy furniture store, and a small side table. A low-hanging light protrudes from the ceiling. I take all my privates in here, unlike Rico, who opts for the velvet rooms around the corner. They're slightly larger but less private. Those rooms have a frosted sliding glass door with no lock. You can't make out what's happening inside, but anyone can bust in on you. The velvet rooms have chaise lounges. Jim figures if the door doesn't lock, we won't take things too far. The booths may be small, but you can do a lot behind that locked door.

I always work in the same room, so DJ Andre has my music playing on a loop. The staging area is packed. When I walk through, I make sure to smile at all of them. I see a regular sipping a glass of champagne in the corner. We make eye contact, and she bites her lower lip. She's on one tonight. She always comes in when she's high. I'll never understand why she pays to spend time with me when she could go to any bar in the city and get a guy to touch her for free.

"How are you tonight, Amber?" I kiss her cheek. "You look beautiful."

You always compliment a paying customer. It's part of the fee.

She kisses my neck and inhales. "You smell good. Why do you always smell so good?"

To hide the smell of fear. "It's for you, beautiful."

She pulls back and pouts. "I couldn't get a spot with you tonight."

"What do you mean?"

Jim always makes space for regulars.

"You're booked." She shrugs and downs her champagne just as Percy comes around the corner.

"Sorry, I'm late." He takes Amber's hand and nods to me, and then they walk to an empty booth.

That little motherfucker.

My booth is next door to the one Percy just entered. The door is closed, so my client must be waiting inside. I hope she's worth an extra two hundred because that's what she cost me. Amber is a big tipper, and she expects big things in return. Percy can't compete with me, with or without the pump. He'll be lucky to get fifty bucks.

I'm plotting revenge on him when I step into my booth.

"How are you tonight?" I say without making eye contact.

Next to the door is a little card with her information, how much time she paid for, the negotiated fee, and her name.

"Is this your first time at our club, Leeann?"

"Uh, yeah."

I look up at the sound of her voice.

Sitting in the blue velvet chair is *Leeyan*, not Leeann. The Leeyan who broke Theo's heart. Her hair is short, the ends tinted pink. She looks thinner, healthier than the last time we stood face to face. The day she left.

"What are you doing here?" I lock the door. "How did you know I worked here?"

"I googled you."

There's a chance she didn't see Theo. If she had I doubt she'd be sitting in my booth wearing jeans, a loose-fitting white sleeveless shirt with a black bra, and leather boots. She's dressed up. This was planned.

"Are you really my private?"

She pretends to settle into the chair and crosses her legs. Her red lips shimmer under the dim light. "I booked you for the night."

I check the card still in my hand. "This says you booked fifteen minutes."

"Check the other cards. Alice, Rosalie, Bella"—she smirks—"all me."

"I wouldn't peg you for a *Twilight* fan."

She looks impressed. Most women are.

"It's market research," I explain. *Twilight* was one of the few series I liked. "The books are so much better than the movies."

"Wow, you're good." She points at me. "So, are we doing this?"

"Don't you think we should talk?"

"Is that normal?"

"Nothing about this is normal."

She seems really nonchalant about being here. Classic Leeyan. She's almost as good at role-playing as I am. She had everyone convinced she was happy about becoming a mother right up until the day she ran away and joined the army.

"I don't feel comfortable dancing for you."

"Fair enough." She stands up. "Let's eat."

If there was ever a time to eat my feelings, it's now.

"Does Theo know you're back?"

"Not yet. I have a plan." She takes a step closer.

I'm flat against the door. "Was this part of your plan?"

"I just want to talk. We're good at that, remember?"

She's referring to the night on the roof. The night we don't speak of.

Black Wednesday.

Leeyan Flores wrecked my best friend, abandoned her daughter, and indirectly derailed my life. She's the last person on earth I should be meeting at a bar, yet, I can't find the will to say no.

I tell Leeyan to meet me at the Lucky Charm, a dive bar down the street. I shower and change out of my G-string, praying Theo doesn't come to the locker room while I'm here. If I don't see him, I won't have to lie to him. Informing him his ex is back in town is the last thing I want to do.

"Dude," Thor rumbles from outside the door. "I just made six bills on a lap dance. Let's hit up that after-hours spot."

"Can't do it." I open the bathroom door and look around the locker room. "Is Theo back?"

"No. He's working the floor." Thor frowns. "Why not? You have a hot date?"

"Nobody says 'hot date' anymore."

"Fuck you." He takes off his sweats and smells them. "You're nasty."

"The chick smelled like watermelon." He holds his dirty pants out toward my face. "Check it out."

"Get the fuck away from me!"

I step into my Jordan's and grab my cell. "I gotta bounce."

I open the door to leave, and Dain walks in.

"Are we hanging out tonight?" Dain tosses a towel in the dirty bin. It misses, and he leaves it on the floor.

"Pretty boy has a date. It's not hot though." Thor wraps a towel around his naked waist. "I'm free."

"Come on, Gio—I'm buying the first round." Dain holds up four hundred-dollar bills.

Everybody made money tonight. Technically, I did too, but it's dirty money. It's Leeyan's money.

"I hooked that tech executive," I lie. They'll never know. "See you when the stock market crashes."

I'm walking toward the Lucky Charm, feeling anxious, like I'm going to meet a date—and not a "date" date, a real date, as in someone who isn't paying for my time...even though Leeyan did buy me for the night.

This is all kinds of fucked up.

The Lucky Charm is a pit and hardly ever busy. Unlike the other bars on Broadway, they don't have a DJ spinning on the weekends. This place is for drinking, and that's what I plan to do.

I sit beside Leeyan and order a Jameson. The barely legal Asian female bartender places a shot in front of me.

I toss it back and motion for another. "Double."

She pours it and walks away.

"So." Leeyan sips her beer.

"So."

"We should talk."

"About what?"

We're both facing the wall of bottles. If someone walked in, we could be two strangers sitting at a bar.

"Then I think it's time we clear the air. We never...the last time I saw you was the day before I shipped out. You called me a selfish cunt and wished me dead."

"I don't remember it like that."

Lie. I remember that day clearly. When Theo left the room to get Lulu's stuffed elephant, I laid into Leeyan. Told her she was evil and didn't deserve happiness.

"Do you remember Cookie?"

"Ah, Cookie." I hold my up glass in a toast to her.

After Theo started dating Leeyan, I decided fucking Cookie was the answer to my pent-up frustration. I didn't think it would take nearly three years for her to finally cave. Cookie played hard to get but eventually crumbled.

"She wrote to me about you." Leeyan pretends to be appalled. "She thought you were in love with her."

"We slept together three times, once in a port-o-potty—that's not true love."

"Come on, you sent ten dozen flowers on her birthday."

The flowers sealed the deal— ten dozen cheap daisies and her panties came flying off. At that point, I was working with Rico, and women were paying top dollar for my dick. Cookie was my last conquest.

"She should've given it up sooner and saved us both the drama."

Leeyan shakes her head in disapproval, but she has no right to shame me. If anything, she deserves a little grief.

"Are you excited to see Lulu?"

The mention of her daughter causes a crease in her forehead.

"Honestly, no. I'm scared to death."

"Lulu is pretty scary. You have to watch everything you say around her—she's like a narc."

"When I left, she was barely talking. Now she's a little person. I'm afraid of what she'll ask me. What if I don't have the right answers?"

"Don't worry, Lulu has an answer for everything. She's like a genius kid."

Leeyan looks proud as if she has anything to do with Lulu's intelligence. She may have fifty percent of Leeyan's DNA, but Lulu is all Theo.

"Tell me something else about her."

"Like what?"

"What does she look like?" Leeyan bends down to rummage through her backpack. "This is the last picture I have."

The picture is at least two years old; I can tell because Lulu and Theo are posing in front of my old car.

"She looks the same, I guess. Her hair is longer." I give it back. "I always thought she favored Theo, but now that I see you, there's definitely a resemblance." I don't know why I feel the need to spare her feelings. Leeyan is the enemy. In no universe is this appropriate, the two of us drinking in a bar like civilized people. Every word out of my mouth is a betrayal to Theo. He should be here, not me.

"How did I draw the short straw? Why come to see me?"

"I knew where you stood with me. You were a safe bet."

"I don't get it."

"Cookie, for instance. I stopped writing her two years ago. I probably lost her friendship, and I don't want to confirm it. I'd rather go on believing we're still cool, unlike you..."

"I was a safe bet because I already hated you."

"Exactly." She toasts to that.

I shoot the rest of my whiskey then wave the bartender over for another round.

"How is Theo?" She asks timidly.

This is my chance to be a good friend since he's probably going to disown me when he finds out Leeyan came to see before him and Lulu.

"He's killing it. He has a great job. Lulu's going to a fancy prep school in the fall. His life is golden."

"Good." She tries not to sound bitter. "I mean that's great. He's okay. I'm glad."

Neither of us believes the words coming out of her mouth.

She runs her fingers through the condensation on her glass. "What about you? Are you golden?"

How I am is none of her business. She's trying to drag me back to the Oasis.

"We're not friends, Leeyan."

"Apparently." She sips her beer.

"I don't get you." I turn to face her. "Shouldn't you be on Theo's doorstep begging to see your daughter?"

She takes a larger drink from her glass. Holds it in her mouth, then swallows. She doesn't look at me when she speaks.

"I didn't tell anyone on base I had a daughter. If I had, they would ask about her, and I wouldn't know what to say because I don't know anything about her. The truth is, I stopped writing. I told myself it didn't matter because Lulu was too young to read. I stopped calling. I figured Lulu didn't remember what I looked like, let alone the sound of my voice. Eventually, enough time passed that I started to believe they were better off without me."

Her confession chips away at the armor I built to prevent her from getting to me. Hating her was the only way I knew how to deal with the pain of losing something I never really had. Leeyan was the first and last woman I have ever truly desired. When I saw my best friend dancing with her, I knew he felt the same way.

Theo couldn't wait to introduce me to the girl he met at Oasis on Black Wednesday. The girl he met the night I was running late. I left the club and texted Theo that I couldn't find parking. Everything would have been fine if Theo didn't bring her to my parents' house the day after Thanksgiving. I played it off like we hadn't met. She rolled with the lie until Theo went to the bathroom and we were alone in the kitchen. She asked me why I didn't show. I pulled a mask on and told her something else came up. Something better. She believed the lie. I think that hurt more than watching Theo fall in love with her.

Leeyan never cared about me. The night on the roof was dwindled down to an insignificant conversation between two people who barely knew each other. It's remained buried in the depths of my subconscious, until now.

"Just because you lied to a bunch of strangers doesn't mean you had to cut Theo off. He waited for over a year for you to write, call, something."

"I fucked up." Her voice cracks. "You want me to admit it, I will. I fucked up, and now all I can do is pray my daughter will forgive me. I've given up any fantasies I had about reconciling with Theo. We never should have been together in the first place." She looks up at me. "We weren't meant to be." I sense a double-meaning in her statement.

I limited my interactions with Leeyan once she became a permanent part of Theo's life. I converted the pain and jealousy that manifested every time they kissed or held hands, into hatred. I slept with all her friends and flaunted my conquests in her face. In some fucked way, I should thank Leeyan. If it weren't for her falling in love with my best friend, I wouldn't be the man I am today. I tell myself I dodged a bullet. Too bad my best friend took the hit for me.

Even though Leeyan has been the enemy for years, I feel myself weakening in her presence. I can't afford to get sloppy. Leeyan uses feelings as ammunition. She manipulated her way into Theo's life, trapped him with a kid, then bailed. She's the kind of woman with the power to blow a motherfucker up. I feel like any minute she's going to spray with me with gas and light a match.

"I saw him at the club."

Theo working at Trance isn't a secret, but I highly doubt it's something he would brag about to Leeyan.

"I wouldn't have recognized him if it wasn't for the tattoo of Lulu's name on his forearm. I assume you're the one responsible for his transformation."

"If you're asking if I'm the one who turned him into a beast, then yes."

The bartender brings Leeyan another beer. She downs what is left in her current glass then swaps the empty glass for the full one.

"I'm not into muscles."

"All women are into muscles."

"Not me."

"I guess you're not into men anymore."

Leeyan only dated women before she met Theo. He was her first male sexual partner. Had I known she still had her v-card the night on the roof, things may have gone differently. That's the lie I tell myself. I wouldn't even kiss her. Out of all the women I'd met before her, none scared me the way Leeyan did. I haven't allowed myself to be that vulnerable since the night on the roof.

"We both know I'm attracted men."

She's trying to bait me into talking about the roof. I keep playing dumb. It's my specialty.

"I love who I love, male or female."

"As long as they don't have muscles." I flex my arm.

She squeezes it and says, "Very firm."

My cock twitches.

"Did you love anyone in Germany?"

"No," she huffs.

I give her side-eye as I hold the glass to my lips.

"All work and no play?"

"You have no idea."

Not many women can pull off a demure grin, but Leeyan Flores has mastered it. I don't want to notice these things about her, but...whiskey.

"How about Theo? Does he love anyone?"

I think of Sylvie, his babysitter with benefits. I don't know their status these days. "You'll have to ask him."

"Is that a yes?" She seems concerned—jealous.

"What Theo does and doesn't do with his dick is not my concern."

"Dicks have nothing to do with love."

"Oh, then you must be talking about that thing pumping blood to my dick." My dick perks up when he hears me refer to him.

Leeyan is like one of those frequency scramblers, fucking up the reception around her. My brain doesn't know what to think. My body doesn't know what it feels, what it wants. I search for a spark of the loathing and animosity I felt for her three years ago. The only thing I find is the bottom of my glass. I set it on the bar and motion for the bartender.

Leeyan knocks her knee against my leg as she spins to face me.

"How about I buy you a shot?"

"Sure, why not."

"Tequila?" She hits my knee a second time.

The perfect igniter.

She orders two shots of reposado while I fidget with the corner of my napkin. This is not how a typical date goes for me. This is not a date. This is me about to go up in flames. If anyone can create hell on earth, it's Leeyan.

A small glass with clear alcohol is placed in front of me along with a dried lemon wedge.

"I'm going to drink until I hate you again." She holds up her glass in salute then tosses it back.

"I still hate you." I take my shot and slam the glass on the bar.

Neither of us wants to show weakness by using the lemon.

The bartender refills my whiskey glass, though I really want water.

Fuck that—I'm not drinking water when she's still got a beer.

"What are we doing here, Leeyan?"

"I was discharged," she replies in a matter-of-fact tone. "So, I came home."

"This isn't home." I twist to face her, resting my elbow on the bar. I'm a little heated and not sure who I'm supposed to be right now. I'm not in work mode, not in date mode, so who am I here?

She takes her time before speaking. Leeyan is calculating, conniving. I should only trust fifty percent of the words that leave her mouth.

My eyes drift to her mouth.

She doesn't bite her lip, smirk, or smile. Her slightly parted lips are tinted a soft raspberry red. Other than a little mascara, she doesn't appear to be wearing makeup, at least not the level of foundation and contouring I'm used to seeing on women. Leeyan looks natural, clean like she just got out of the army.

"I was scared to go home, and since I don't have anyone else..." She shrugs and takes a mouthful of beer. "You're the safe bet."

"How did you even know I was working tonight?'

"Fred told me." She makes a squiggly line in the condensation built up on her glass.

"Fred, as in my doorman, Fred?"

"I went by your place, but you weren't home."

It worries me that she doesn't see this as stalkerish. I definitely need to have a talk with Fred about privacy.

"Don't get me wrong..." She speaks with her whole body. Her hands fly up in defense. "I want to see Lulu. She's the reason I came back. But showing up at ten o'clock at night didn't seem like the right time."

"Probably not."

"Had I known Theo wasn't going to be home, I might have reconsidered. Who is taking care of Lulu tonight?"

"She's with the babysitter, Sylvie. Don't worry, she has a son, so she's got experience or whatever."

I'm babbling. I'm tipsy, and I'm babbling. I need food.

Leeyan does a slow nod like she's trying to figure out if I'm lying.

"Does Theo work every night?"

"Just Friday through Sunday."

She pretends to be impressed. "You guys must make decent money. Shit, I paid two-fifty for thirty minutes."

"That can't be right." I shake my head. "My fee is two fifty for fifteen minutes."

Leeyan's face turns red as she starts to laugh.

"What's so funny?"

"I might have lied about buying you for the night."
She guzzles her beer. "I only bought one dance."

"What do you mean? I saw the cards, the names..." A
light bulb explodes above my head. "You faked the cards."

"I'm sorry!" She continues to laugh. "They were
sitting on the counter for anyone to grab. The club really
needs better security."

Reality sinks in—I didn't make any money tonight. I
can't afford to slack. I might have considered going back
to the club, but I'm too drunk. Jim and his fucking rules.
We can drink while we work, but getting wasted is bad for
business, mostly because drunk strippers and drunk
patrons usually end up having drunk sex in bathrooms.
Leeyan has cost me at least six hundred dollars tonight
and possibly my best friend.

"You're the fucking devil."

"Quit being dramatic." She elbows me in the ribs.

"Ouch."

"Sorry." She rubs her hand down my back. "Did I
hurt your vagina?"

I push her away but can't help smiling. Being around
her isn't horrible. "What am I doing here?"

"Talking, drinking." She lifts her almost empty glass.

"You're going to cost me my best friend, again." I pull
out my wallet and set it on the table, the universal sign that
I'm ready to go.

She places her hand over mine. "The last time I was
honest about my feelings was on the roof, with you."

I stare at her hand on mine and wish it didn't make
me feel some kind of way.

"Can we just be two people who get each other? No past, no animosity—can we be that?" She shifts so her chest is pressed against my arm. It doesn't feel intentionally sexual. I can't assume every woman wants sex from me. For once in my life, sex is the last thing I'm thinking about when I look at Leeyan.

"So, you want to be friends?" I confirm.

"Just friends." She smiles and rests her head on my shoulder for a brief second before scooting back to her space.

Being friends sounds good, but it's tainted by the fact that I already have a friend and a good one at that.

"I can't lie to him—not about this."

"Can you avoid mentioning I'm back? At least until I figure out my next move. I want to have a plan before I drop in on their lives. I don't want to be my mom"

Leeyan's mom was an addict. I don't know the details but Theo mentioned it as one reason Leeyan is so fucked up.

"When I was a kid, not much older than Lulu, my mom would leave me with my godmother, Louisa, for days. She always came back with promises and fairytales of us moving into our own place. A big house on a hill or a cabin in the woods. I would pack all our things into a big black garbage bag and drag it to the front door. I'd sit there all day into the night. Louisa would try to convince me to go to bed. I wouldn't move. I didn't want to risk her coming back and me not being there. I refuse to do that to Lulu. I don't want to bounce in and out of her life. When I go back, it's for good."

"You're not your mother," I say this with enough conviction for her to believe it too.

She smiles like she might agree. "Give me two weeks. I swear you won't regret it."

Admitting I'm the biggest hypocrite on the planet isn't at the top of my priority list. I've spent years telling Theo he's better off without Leeyan, and now I'm in a secret alliance with her.

It's almost one in the morning, Theo has to be home by now. I deem it safe enough to stop by the cheesesteak shop for a quick sandwich. Leeyan wolfs down her sandwich along with half my fries. I can't recall the last time I shared a meal with a woman. The dinners I attend with clients usually consist of booze and a salad; I'm usually the main course and dessert. Maybe it's the whiskey but sitting next to Leeyan doesn't freak me out as much as I thought it would. She makes me feel comfortable like this isn't a big deal or a major betrayal. It almost feels like the night on the roof.

A soft mist covers the street as we leave the cheesesteak place. I put my jacket on and pull my keys out.

"Where are you staying?"

She points to the hostel down the street.

"Why are you staying there?"

She pulls a green army hoodie from her backpack. "It's cheap."

We start walking toward the Green Tortoise Hostel.

"Do you have a private room?"

"Nah, I'm used to sharing." She points to where 'ARMY' is printed across her chest.

"Do they know you're military?"

"I don't think places like the Green Tortoise give military discounts."

We stop in front of the bright green building, where four kids sit on the sidewalk near the door vaping.

"Good night?" one of them says, his accent making it sound like he's asking a question.

"Good night," Leeyan replies with a friendly smile. "They're from Brazil."

The mention of my exit strategy is like a small reality check. I'll be gone in a few months. Once Leeyan integrates herself back into Theo and Lulu's life, he won't need me anymore.

I shove my hands into my pocket. "It's freezing."

She looks up at the building. "I can't have guests."

I wasn't expecting to be invited inside. She must have considered it.

That causes a twitch in my pants. Leeyan has a big red 'no fucking' sign over her head. Like a horny teenager, knowing I can't have her makes me think otherwise. I won't deny feeling comfortable around her, but my couch is comfortable, too, and that doesn't mean I want to fuck it.

"I know you want time but I really think you should at least contact Theo and let him know you're planning to come back." Bringing up Theo is a boner-killer.

"I will." She hugs herself. "I just need to work up the balls to do it."

"You have no balls."

"I wish I did. Then you could kick me in the balls and make me go see them."

"Why is this on me?"

"You said we were friends."

"And that somehow obligated me to be your official ball-kicker?"

"You look like you've kicked some balls in your day." She socks my arm. "Don't worry, I won't let any of this blow back on you."

My dick hears the words 'blow on you' and gets excited. I need to get as far away as possible. Drunk Gio makes terrible choices. I pull a business card from my pocket and hand it to Leeyan.

"This has my cell phone number. Text me tomorrow if you grow some balls."

"Thanks, Gio." She places the card in the back pocket of her jeans.

We stand on the sidewalk awkwardly shivering.

"Good night?" the Brazilian says again. This time his tone is clear.

I look at him over Leeyan's head and reply.

"*Sem boa noite.*"

The four guys let out a collective "oh." They're clearly impressed with my language skills and start yelling things in Portuguese. I recognize a few phrases, like "Kiss her!" and "She wants you."

"What did you say?" Leeyan is stunned.

"I said good night. Actually, I said it's *not* a good night."

She looks offended. "I should go inside." She opens the front door.

Am I supposed to hug her? Shake her hand, give her a high five?

This is why I don't date.

This is not a date, but if it were, I'd be blowing it.

Or better yet, she'd be blowing me.

"I'm going." I start walking away.

"Later," she yells.

I turn to wave and see a naked man run out the front door. He shoves Leeyan out of his way before face-planting on the sidewalk. His ass is red as if someone beat him with a belt.

A sizeable Asian male exits the building holding a stick, the kind a ninja would carry, and he's yelling at him in another language. Sirens approach as two police cars fly up the street. People start to file out of the hostel.

"What happened?" Leeyan asks a girl with blonde dreads.

"He broke into one of the female dorms and started jerking off while the girls were sleeping."

"Is he a guest?" I ask.

"No, he snuck in through the back." She lights a joint. "And they found a hidden camera in the third-floor bathroom."

"Go get your shit," I tell Leeyan. "You're staying with me."

CHAPTER FIVE

I'm not a nice guy. I don't do nice things for people. So, why I am sitting in my apartment with Theo's baby mama?

She returns from the bathroom wearing gray sweatpants and sits beside me. The cool temperature of my apartment is visible through her green army t-shirt. She's the first woman, besides Antonia, that I've had in my apartment. This place is my sanctuary. No masks, no role play. I can eat and jerk off in privacy.

I'm trying to play it cool like her very presence isn't a trigger. My cock is a trained seal, and being within twenty feet of a bed or any fuckable surface with a woman gets his attention.

"What are we drinking?" she asks.

Drinking is a bad idea, but I get up and go to the kitchen anyway. I open and close cabinets like I don't live here. I take this opportunity to school my dick on what is happening.

Leeyan isn't my type. I jerk off to curvy women with big fake tits, fake eyelashes, and long, possibly fake hair. My ideal woman is fake.

Leeyan is real. I can smell her from across the room. She reeks of coconut and jasmine.

"Uh, I have Jameson or a bottle of merlot."

"Do you even have to ask?"

I grab two glasses and the bottle of Jameson, set the glasses on the coffee table, and fill them a quarter full.

She watches me pour. "I probably shouldn't drink anymore tonight."

"Me either," I agree before taking a large sip.

Leeyan holds her glass with both hands like a child holding a mug of hot cocoa. "Do you have someplace to be tomorrow?"

It's Saturday. I usually hit the gym around ten then come home to shower and manscape before going to the club. Trance is the last place I want to be. There is no way to explain this to Theo. He's waited years for Leeyan to return. The night it finally happens, she doesn't even call him. I'd rather sit naked on a chair made of thumbtacks than tell my best friend the love of his life is crashing on my couch.

"Not really. Just some errands."

"Good." She blushes. "Then I'm not totally fucking up your life."

Yet.

As I see it, this can only get worse. I should get rid of her, send her back to the hostel where she will most likely be raped and murdered. If I have to choose between Theo's feelings and Leeyan's life, I'd say I'm doing the right thing.

Leeyan brings the glass to her mouth and stares at me over the rim. She's comfortable here, I can feel it, but I don't know why.

"I can't get that big red ass out of my mind."

I offer a small laugh. "Some things can't be unseen."

"I bet you've seen some interesting things."

I grin and nod.

"Tell me something."

"Like what?"

"The craziest thing you've seen at the club."

"No way."

"Why, embarrassed?" She nudges my leg with her toes.

I look down at her bare foot.

"Line. Crossing." I draw an imaginary line between us.

She pulls her foot back. "Sorry," she huffs.

"And what happens in the club stays in the club."

She drinks to that. "How long has Theo worked at Trance?"

It doesn't feel right talking about him, but what the hell else am I going to talk about with Leeyan?

"A few months."

"The last I remember he was working for a dog groomer."

It was a shit job with shit pay, but Theo had no choice. Trance was his big break, I won't let Leeyan make him feel bad about making good money.

"Sway...er...Theo is becoming a pretty big attraction at Trance."

"Sway?" Laughter bubbles up and out. "Oh my god, is that his stage name?"

"First, it was my idea. Second, he does whatever it takes to provide for Lulu. If that means dancing for money...he gets the job done."

Leeyan stops laughing to sip her whiskey. "Theo isn't as fragile as you think. You don't need to protect him."

"I know—he's a beast in the gym." I pretend she's referring to his outer strength.

"There are two sides to every story." She sets her glass on the table.

Maybe it's time I heard her side of the story.

"Truth?" I ask.

"Truth or dare?"

"Truth or drink."

She raises an eyebrow.

I top off our glasses. Leeyan places a throw pillow in front of her, hugging it to her chest.

I start with an easy one.

"Was Theo the first man you had sex with?" "Yes." She takes a sip. "He was the first man I was with. My first, first was named Yvette. We did it in a hot tub." She recalls it fondly.

"Do you want to share some of the intimate details?"

That's my dick talking.

"Not going to happen. Since we're on the topic, who was your first?"

I take a drink.

"Weak," she moans.

"How many men have you been with?"

Leeyan is cautious this time. She raises the glass to her lips in contemplation then lowers it. "One."

"One?"

"Did I stutter?"

If Theo was the first and she's only had one, that means...

"I've only been with Theo," she confirms.

"I call bullshit."

"Call it whatever you want. I wasn't into men until Theo, and I haven't found a man I want since him."

"What about a woman?"

She holds up her hand. "It's my turn to ask a question."

"Fair enough." I tilt my glass to her.

Her smile falters, and she clears her throat. I have a feeling the next question isn't going to be easy to answer.

"Do you think I still have a chance with Theo? I'm not saying I want him back. I don't know what I want, but Theo has this power over me. When I see him..."

"Pussy power."

"What?"

"In your case, it's dick power. He gave you something you can't find anywhere else—magic dick."

My dick is begging to make a case for his notable qualities.

"You know him better than anyone—do you think he still cares about me?" Leeyan stares into her glass.

That first year Theo was devout. He played the proud boyfriend of a military woman. I think he joined a Facebook support group. Although, he'd never admit that to me. I tried like hell to get him back in the game but all my attempts to get him laid failed. He did have a toddler, but you can always make time for pussy.

"Honestly, I don't know what Theo is thinking these days. I can tell you it took years for him to stop caring." *Not that he ever did.* "He's a good guy. If nothing else, he'll forgive you."

"Thanks for your honesty." She touches my knee.

My dick notices.

Leeyan isn't thinking about *my* dick, and that fact shouldn't feel like a blow to my ego. By ego, I mean dick. He doesn't know what's going on.

Leeyan is just a friend—an un-fuckable friend.

"I'm not counting that as a question." I squirm, and she removes her hand. "Ask me another one."

"Do you have sex for money or pleasure?"

Not only do I drink, I down my entire glass.

"You can't keep drinking," she challenges.

"The only question you answered was about Theo."

"Who said this game was fair?" I refill my glass. "What about women? Have you been with any since you left Theo?"

She sighs like the question is lame but doesn't hesitate to answer.

"A few, but they were casual encounters."

"Drunken mistakes," I clarify.

"Exactly." She wets her lips with whiskey. "When was the last time you had sex for pleasure?"

I don't care who you are or what kind of relationship you have with a woman when she uses the words "sex" and "pleasure" in the same sentence, it does something to a man.

She wants to fuck you, my dick insists.

I would believe him if this wasn't Leeyan.

Fucking Leeyan is off the table.

And the couch.

And the bed.

I feel like Edward trying to read Bella's mind. I always know where I stand—or where I'm lying down—with a woman. There's a mutual understanding when you're being paid. I have no clue what Leeyan is thinking, what she wants.

I haven't been in a position to want for a long time. Even moving to Brazil, I never would've considered it if Antonia didn't make the offer. Everything I do is calculated and planned with someone else's needs in mind. What I want hasn't mattered to anyone, not even me, for a long time.

"You better not take a drink," Leeyan warns. "I answered all your questions. I'm just trying to level the playing field."

Her eyes are playful, a little droopy from the whiskey. I forgot how cute she was. I'm not talking about her body shape or how she presents herself to the world. I mean she's genuinely pretty.

My chest pounds like some romance novel dumb fuck. I can't be Edward—he doesn't have a heartbeat. I'm Jake now, goofy and lusting after a woman he can't have.

"Are we playing a game?"

"Yes." She hesitates when our eyes meet. "It's called truth or drink."

Her fingers curl around the glass.

I want to be that glass.

My dick is out of control.

"You owe me an answer." Her attempt at scowling is ridiculous. She's too drunk to be serious. She makes duck lips to hide her smile, her brows furrow, and she tilts her head to the side like a confused puppy.

"Cookie."

Leeyan launches the pillow at me. "Liar!"

I take her hand before she grabs another pillow. "It's the truth. Cookie was the last woman I fucked for free."

Her eyes widen, and I realize what I've just admitted.

"I overheard some of the women at club bragging about you. I kind of assumed more went on in those rooms than dancing."

"I don't sleep with women in the club. It's forbidden."

"I'm not judging." Her eyes beg to differ.

"It's a side hustle, like a bachelorette party. Sometimes ladies want more." There's no way to make my side game sound legit. At the end of the day, I fuck for money. A lot of money.

"Does Theo?

"No! He's stage only."

She looks disappointed like she was hoping to uncover some dirt. If she does find something, it won't be from me.

"I guess that's good, for Lulu's sake." She adjusts the pillow in her lap. "One shitty parent is bad enough."

"Who said you're a bad parent?"

I did. So many times.

"I found out I was pregnant six days before my ship-out date. I didn't leave my bed for two days. Theo thought I was nervous about boot camp. I was in mourning, mourning the dream that little blue line killed. What kind of mom looks at her baby as a dream-crusher? Not a good one."

"Nobody said life is fair."

She toasts to that. "Since I'm the woman I get all the blame. It's my body, my choice. That's bullshit. I didn't want to get pregnant. I protected myself. I thought I did enough. I should've insisted Theo wear a condom but you know how that goes."

I don't really know how that goes. I always use a condom.

"I didn't want to take the pill, not before boot camp. Diaphragms aren't bullet-proof. In my case, it wasn't sperm-proof either."

I respond with head nods. Nothing I say will add to the conversation. Nothing nice.

"Accidental pregnancies are always the woman's fault. The man is never shamed. They're pitied. *Poor dude, his girl is trapping him. He's on the hook for eighteen years of child support, eighteen years of hell.*"

She's right. I'm guilty of this very thing. I don't know how many times I accused Leeyan on trapping Theo. I always assumed she wanted to get knocked up. Yeah, she boohooed about it, but I thought it was an act.

"As a society, we consider a part-time father an okay person if he pays child support and sees the kid on birthdays and holidays. A woman can never walk away. Not without a lifetime of shame. On the rare occasion a woman doesn't want children, we assume there is something biologically wrong with her. We brand her as selfish, damaged. I'm not saying I wish my daughter was never born," she insists.

"I get where you're coming from. You weren't prepared to be a mother."

She takes a drink from her glass. "It's more than that. I never wanted to be a mother. But when it came time to make *that choice,* I couldn't deny Theo the opportunity to be a father."

Everything in me is saying to believe her. Theo's life changed the moment he found out Leeyan was pregnant. He became a man.

"You think I'm a horrible person," she states.

"No."

"You haven't said very much." Her eyes are lazy from the alcohol.

"It's a lot to take in."

She closes her eyes, cuts me off. "I just want the chance to make it right. Do I at least deserve that?"

"Of course you do." I reach over the line and touch her arm. It relaxes beneath my hand, and she inches closer to the center of the couch, the safe zone. I adjust my cock so it's pointing in the other direction.

Her shoulder leans into the cushion beside me. We stare at each other the way drunks do when they contemplate bad ideas.

My heart races like I'm crouched behind home plate, calling for a fastball when we're one pitch away from winning the game. I place my glass on the table. When I start making baseball analogies—I've had enough.

She sets her glass beside mine. "This has gone so much better than I thought it would."

"You're not as cunty as I thought you'd be."

She kicks me softly. "And you're not the big dick I thought you were."

"Honey, you have no idea how big a dick I can be."

Her eyes dip to my package. I snatch the pillow from her lap and place it in mine before my dick decides to wave hello.

She tries to steal the pillow back.

I block her hand.

A split second later she's on her knees leaning into me, fighting over the pillow. We're laughing like kids—kids who aren't thinking about sex or boundaries. This is uncharted territory for me.

Could this be the friend zone?

"There are like three other pillows—why do you want this one?" I'm hugging the pillow to my chest. She has no chance. Even so, she tugs at the corner as if her life depends on it.

"Because you have it," she taunts. "Plus, I had it first!"

She gives the pillow a good yank and I let it go. She falls onto her back.

"I win!" Her legs flail in the air like a turtle trying to get right side up.

"I let you win."

"That's still a win." She's sassy now. "Manipulating an enemy into conceding is just as good as beating them in combat—army 101." She victoriously settles into her corner of the couch.

We take a few seconds to catch our breath.

She places the pillow behind her head. "I like this, whatever it is."

"It's comfortable," I admit. It's the roof.

"I forgot how easy it was to talk to you."

"It's one of my better traits."

"Women pay for this?" She swirls her finger around. "Just being with you, talking?"

I give her my best smolder. "They pay for this." I lean forward, resting my arms across her legs. "And this." I run my hand up her thigh and hook my thumb in the waistband of her sweats. My dick has full control of the situation.

"How much does this cost?"

"Depends on what happens next."

"Hypothetically speaking, say I wanted to kiss you—does that cost more? Is kissing an a la carte item? Do you even kiss, or is that just in movies?" She rambles, nervously.

"I kiss, not always open mouth. I try to avoid making out. Making out is a time suck. Since I'm being paid by the hour, I skip the foreplay."

"That isn't true," she corrects. "Everything leading up to this was foreplay. Sitting here, talking, touching—all foreplay."

Is she saying what I think she's saying?

"I'm not saying we—this—is foreplay. If I were a client..." She stumbles over her words. "If I were paying for your time, this would be worth every penny."

I'm still leaning over her with my fingers in the waist of her pants. Her breathing accelerates; my balls tighten.

"Maybe we should call it a night." I sit up.

She stops me. "Wait."

A pink strand of hair sticks to her cheek. I want to move it. I want an excuse to touch her. She looks at me extremely vulnerable. That's impossible because Leeyan is strong in every way. Her arms are lean, muscular. Her body is well defined. She probably benches twice her weight. It isn't her outside that's giving me a reaction. It's something else, something more profound.

I care.

Caring is dangerous. Caring leads to feelings. I can't afford to feel right now. I won't let a little whiskey fuck up my life.

"There's a blanket in the closet next to the bathroom."

I stand. "Goodnight, Leeyan."

"Just so you know—" She lays down, taking up the full length of the couch. "—I fully expect to collect my dance."

Her cocky attitude ignites my ego. Leeyan Flores is challenging me, and I never back down from a challenge.

CHAPTER SIX

Sleeping was difficult with Leeyan in the other room. I spent most of the night trying to figure out how I'm going to explain this to Theo. The woman he gave up everything for, the mother of his child, is back.

And she's here with me.

An ordinary woman would've gone straight to her kid. She hasn't seen Lulu in three years; you'd think she would make a beeline from the airport to see her daughter. It's obvious to me now, more than ever, that Leeyan is not a normal woman.

Whose job is it to determine what normalcy should be? Maybe it's normal for Leeyan to be nervous about seeing the daughter she abandoned, or maybe she's a selfish bitch. It isn't my place to judge. My loyalty was always to Theo; he was the victim in the story—that was Theo's story.

Leeyan was a sworn enemy, a shoot-to-kill enemy. Whenever her name would weasel its way into the conversation, a barrage of insults would fly from my mouth like grenades. She was one of those if-I-ever-see-her-on-the-street people, the ones you spend hours verbally abusing in your head. I had a whole hate speech memorized in case our paths ever crossed, but when I saw her sitting in my booth, there wasn't a hateful thought in my mind.

"Gio," she says softly from the hall.

"Yeah," I reply, my voice cracking. I clear my throat and answer again, this time sounding like a man. "Yeah, do you need something?"

"I just wanted to ask if you need to use the bathroom."

"Nah, you go ahead."

"Are you sure? Because I want to take a shower."

I have no clue how long she's going to be, and I have to take a piss.

"Gimme a minute." I jump out of bed, put on my black Armani sweatpants. Leeyan is leaning against the wall just outside the bathroom door, which is right beside my bedroom. She stands at attention when I appear.

"At ease, soldier."

She smiles and goes back to slouching. Her eyes rake over my abs. Having a woman check me out is an everyday occurrence at the club, but not in the hallway of my home.

"I'll just be a sec..." I point to the bathroom behind her.

"Oh shit, sorry." She moves aside. "That...your..." She points at my body. "Those are, uh, stellar." She punches my arm. "Good job."

"Thanks, I try." I watch her face turn ten shades of red as I close the bathroom door. Then I turn red. The compliment was hella awkward.

I'm the kind of guy who believes men and women cannot be friends. The best-case scenario is she gets back together with Theo. Then this would be a lot less complicated.

I don't want that.

Why don't I want that?

Because Theo is a fucked-up human when he's with Leeyan.

I lift the toilet seat and start to pee. Midstream, Leeyan knocks.

What. The. Fuck.

I stop peeing.

"I hope that wasn't weird. I felt like it would be weird not to say something about your body, you know?" She's rambling. "It doesn't really do me any good to pretend I didn't notice your abs. So, if we're being totally normal, acknowledging your body was the normal thing to do, don't you think?"

"Uh, I'm peeing."

"Oh, yeah." She laughs. "I'll wait until you get out."

Her feet slap against the concrete tile as she walks away. "Okay, I'm all the way in the living room, sitting on the couch, in case you're gun shy."

Oh lord.

I finish and decide I need to look somewhat presentable. Bedhead is only cute when you share a bed. I wet my hair then brush my teeth. This isn't for her; it's for me.

Mostly.

When I finish, I find Leeyan in the kitchen, trying to make coffee.

"Do you have filters?" She opens the cabinet where the plates and bowls are kept.

"No, it doesn't need one." I step behind her, trapping her between me and the counter. I open the top of the coffee pot to show her the metal filter inside.

"Oh, cool."

We both reach for the coffee container. Our fingers touch like Edward and Bella in the car scene when they both reach for the heater controls. She pulls back then steps to the side.

"I'll just stand here and watch." She leans on the counter.

I place six scoops into the filter then close the top. She's already filled it with water. "It's pretty easy, now you just push this button."

I look up and catch her staring at the tattoos on my arm. I flex slightly when I place the coffee back in its spot.

"Do you, uh, have cream and sugar?"

"Coconut creamer is in the fridge, but no sugar. I have agave." I open the cabinet above her head and remove the bottle. "It's better than sugar."

She smirks at the healthy alternative. "It'll do."

She steps away from the counter, toward the refrigerator as I move toward the door. She sidesteps to the right; I do the same. Then we both step the other way.

"Is this the coffee dance?" She starts sidestepping to an imaginary beat. She waves her arms like the roof is on fire. The chick is mental.

In no way do I think her movements are sexy—until her ass brushes my thigh. The tiniest of sparks ricochets through my body. It feels incestuous, wrong, like the time I flirted with my third cousin at a wedding. She kept hugging me, telling me how cute I was. I jerked off to her for a year. Every time I came to the image of her in that puffy pink bridesmaid dress, I felt like I was one step closer to hell.

"The coffee is going to take ten minutes." I point to the hall. "The bathroom is free."

She winks and makes a clicking sound. "Roger that."

She dances her way out of the kitchen, and I adjust my junk.

What the fuck, dude.

She's Theo's ex.

She's Theo's ex.

She's Theo's ex.

"Towels?" she yells from the bathroom.

"In the cabinet on the right."

Said cabinet squeaks open. "Found them."

The door closes, and the water turns on. I exhale.

Leeyan is a test. If I can keep my dick in check with a woman sleeping on my couch, maybe there's hope for things staying platonic with Antonia.

My future depends on it. If I can't control myself with the most un-fuckable woman in the city, there's no way I'll be able to keep things all business with Antonia.

The bathroom door opens again. "Uh, question."

I walk around the corner. She's standing in the doorway with a towel around her naked body. Her bare shoulders are muscular and sexy as hell.

"Is it cool if I use your shampoo? I just realized I left mine at the hostel."

"Sure, if you don't mind smelling like Swagger."

"I'm all about the swag, baby." She closes the door with a fuckload of swag.

I bang my forehead on the wall.

I go to the kitchen and text Rico to let him know I won't be making it to the gym today.

Leeyan is in the bathroom for almost an hour. I make a mental note to always pee before she showers. Once I finally get my turn in the bathroom, it feels off. Strands of her hair decorate the shower floor; her toothbrush sits in the slot beside mine. The thought of her standing in my shower, naked, turns me on—not enough to fuck her, but just knowing a naked chick was in my shower, rubbing my body wash on her lady parts gives me full-blown wood. I stroke it out and wonder if Leeyan was doing the same thing in here.

Oh damn, I like that visual.

I slap myself in the face.

Get it together, man!

The last thing I want or need is to complicate things any further with Theo. Lusting after his ex-girlfriend breaks several bro codes.

I dress in my least sexy clothes: faded jeans and a baggy orange Giants t-shirt. Leeyan is sitting at my computer wearing jeans with a heather gray crewneck sweatshirt. Her sleeves are pushed up to her elbows.

"What's on the agenda today?" I sit on the couch to put on my socks. "I'm pretty sure Theo is home with Lulu."

Leeyan covers her face and moans. "I'm so scared to see her. What if she hates me?"

"She's too young to harbor long-term hate."

"Maybe." She shrugs. "I know Theo hates me, which is fine because I kind of hate him too."

As fucked up as their relationship is, they still have Lulu. The kid always comes first.

"I think you should go see Lulu. If you want, I can talk to Theo."

I don't want to, but I will for the kid.

"No, the last thing you need is to be in the middle."

Too late.

"I just need a few days to get my head straight, find my own place, grow some balls." She takes her coffee mug to the sink.

Leeyan catches my eye from across the apartment. I don't look away. It feels like we're having a moment—a teaching moment.

"Are you going to rinse that?"

She looks down at the sink. "Am I supposed to rinse it?"

"Yes. Then put it in the dishwasher."

"What if I want more coffee later?"

"You get a new mug."

"That seems wasteful."

"It's hygienic."

"But then you have to wash two mugs."

"*I* don't. The dishwasher cleans them, and it doesn't care if there are two mugs or twenty."

"How often do you run the dishwasher?" She folds her arms and leans against the counter.

"Every day."

"You have like two things in there."

"It's early—it'll fill up throughout the day."

"O-kay."

I show her where the dishwasher pods are stored and how to empty the coffee grounds.

"Does the coffee filter go in the dishwasher?"

"No," I grunt. "You rinse it with warm, soapy water." I point at the sponge. "Any other questions?"

"About cleaning, no."

I hope my good cleaning habits rub off on her. That's the only thing I'll be rubbing off on her.

I sit at my desk and open my email. I have two new messages, one is from the Agency with a last-minute booking for tonight. I have to take it since I made no money last night. The other email is from Antonia. It contains links to apartments and information on the work permits and visas.

Leeyan sits on the sofa with the newspaper. Her daughter, whom she hasn't seen in three years is a twenty-minute Uber ride away, and she's reading the comics.

"Do you have any plans for today?" I ask.

"I'm working on one."

"Reading the comics is part of your plan?"

She closes the paper and looks back at me. "I'm waiting to hear back on a few apartments, and I emailed a contact who might have a job for me."

"Cool." I play it off like I don't really care.

"Can I read the comics without judgment now, please?"

"No judgment here."

She watches me a few seconds before opening the paper.

Nice to know she has a plan. I need one too. An exit plan because there is no way this ends well. I click on the link to start my visa application.

CHAPTER SEVEN

I arrive at a warehouse in Dogpatch. It's a former blue-collar area with million-dollar homes on one side of Third Street and warehouses on the other. I park in the lot along with half a dozen Audis and Jettas. I fit right in.

Music pumps from inside the building; it sounds like a rave. If there were more cars in the lot, it'd feel like a rave. I check the text from Rico to make sure this is the place. The address is correct. He didn't give any details about the job, just said private party, which usually means an hour of dancing and I'm out. I'm not up for more. I spent most of the day stress eating with Leeyan.

A woman appears in a stairwell on the side of the building. She lights a cigarette and blows smoke toward the exposed light above the door. A pink robe covers the top half of her body, and a strange crown sits on her head. It looks like a balloon tiara, the sort of thing a clown makes for a kid.

"Are you Giovanni?" a male voice calls from the front door.

She looks down from her perch, smoke seeping from her mouth when she smiles at me.

"Yeah." I walk toward the man, hoping he's not the job.

Rico knows my limits. I don't fuck men, and I don't let them suck me off or touch me. Dancing for them is okay. I'll do a birthday party for a dude, but it's a hands-off event.

"I'm Gilby." He extends his hand. "Call me Gil."

Like the woman on the stairs, Gil is tall, slender, and blond. From his slight accent, he's most likely German.

Gil leads me into the warehouse. It's a large open space with a metal staircase leading to an observation deck surrounding a large open area filled with balloons. It reminds me of Oasis. If it weren't for the twenty half-naked adults, this place could be mistaken for Chuck E. Cheeses or some other annoying kid-friendly establishment.

After a quick scan around the place, it's clear I wasn't hired as entertainment. I'm not even the best-looking guy in the room—the darkest, yes, but not the most handsome. That title would go to the six-six blond dude with ice blue eyes and a chiseled six-pack. For a guy who takes his clothes off for a living, I'm feeling a little self-conscious around this crowd.

"Have you heard of looners?" Gil hands me a bottle of Hefeweizen.

I don't usually drink wheat beer, but I doubt they have Guinness.

"I don't think so." I nod my thanks for the beer.

"Looners are people who find balloons arousing."

Wait, what?

He picks up a long red balloon. "This is an airship."

The oblong shape looks like a blimp.

"It's made of a special material so it's durable." He squeezes the airship until the sides are smashed together then places it on the ground, slips out of his loafer, and steps on it.

"It seems very durable." I have no fucking clue how someone can get off on a balloon. "Do you like, rub on it?"

"You fuck on it." He certainly gets to the point. "Women like to bounce on them. It depends on the person."

Balloons or no balloons, this feels like an orgy. That costs extra.

"And how do I fit into this?"

Gil laughs and calls someone to join us. "Runa, love, come."

The woman from the stairwell outside appears from the other side of the balloon pit. Her pink robe is gone, and she struts toward us in a black lace bra and high-waisted panties. Garters hold up fishnet stockings, and the only thing missing is a pair of stilettos. Like most of the people in the building, she's shoeless.

"Runa, this is Giovanni from The Agency."

"Nice to meet you." Her hand is cold and soft, traces of her cigarette wafting into my nostrils when she leans in to kiss my cheek.

I pray to the sex gods that I get to fuck Runa on a balloon tonight.

"Giovanni, do you know how to use one of these?"

Gil pulls a camcorder out of a duffel bag.

"Uh, yeah, but we have a no camera rule, and that includes video." As much as I'd love to watch the playback of Runa riding me on top of that red airship, it's forbidden.

Runa and Gil laugh.

"No, no. You're mistaken. We aren't filming you. You are here to film us." Gil pulls Runa into his arms, staking claim.

The chatter around the room softens as the music dies down.

"So, you need me to play cameraman?"

"Yes."

"I walk around filming you guys doing...what you do?"

"Come on." Gil leads me up the stairs to a tripod holding a camera. "We have cameras set up all around the warehouse to catch us at various angles from above. We need you down there, up close."

"Do you mind if I ask why you hired someone from The Agency for this job?"

"Our regular man had to cancel last minute—he was hired to film a private event for Elon Musk, and he pays more than we do." Gil laughs. "Rico understands the importance of discretion."

"That we do."

"Wear this." He hands me a beanie and a pair of dark glasses. "You'll be caught on film from these cameras, and I assume you want to keep your identity hidden."

"Should I avoid your faces?"

They have a lot of cameras set up for people who don't want to be seen.

"We aren't ashamed of what we do. The secrecy isn't about our identity—it's for the movie. People will pay to watch this, so we can't have it leaking on YouTube, you know?"

Fetishes are a huge online business. People pay a lot of money to watch kinky shit.

"You're good now?" Gil sets his hand on my shoulder.

"Yes, I'm good."

My dick is disappointed we won't be participating, but I'm good with being paid two grand to film a gang of Nordic supermodels fucking balloons.

We go back downstairs. Gil gives me some quick pointers on what people want to see and the angles I should film.

"It's okay to run from one person to another. Make sure you get everyone. Some key shots will be foreplay. Viewers get off on watching us inflate the balloons. You must also get shots of bouncing."

"Bouncing?"

"Yes, bouncing. Runa show him, darling."

Runa chooses a black balloon shaped like a light bulb and smiles at me as she straddles it with the narrow part protruding between her sexy-as-fuck legs. She slowly starts to bounce, the way a woman does when she sits on your dick. Her head falls backward, and she moans like it's the best ride of her life—just from bouncing on a balloon.

"Let's get started," someone yells. "You're killing us, Gil!"

The crowd shouts agreements in English and another language that sounds like German or Swedish.

"There are more cameras there"—Gil points to a table in the corner—"in case the battery dies. Don't forget your disguise, unless you want your face on video."

I pull the beanie on and test the glasses. The lenses are dark, but the room seems relatively clear.

"Any questions?"

I shake my head.

"Great, I'll go change the music." Gil starts back up the stairs then stops. "Don't stay on one person too long." He finds Runa in the crowd. "She's beautiful, yes?"

"Yes."

"She's my wife, and we don't fuck other people."

Noted.

Gil puts on Bjork's "It's Oh So Quiet," the strange theatrical tune making the scene almost comical as the lighting flickers red, blue, yellow, and orange. People remove what little clothing they have on. Nobody is fully nude, just panty-less under a skirt or lace lingerie.

Runa and Gil remain in their fancy underwear.

I walk around holding the camera waist high, shooting hands caressing these massive balloons. One dude takes a deflated balloon and rubs it between a woman's legs. She's spread eagle on a green airship. I zoom close, so close I see her wetness on the black latex. After a few minutes he lowers his mouth. Instead of licking her crotch, he wraps his lips around the balloon and starts to blow it up.

The woman loses her shit.

I make sure to get her face in the shot. Her red lipstick smears over her cheek as she thrashes in pleasure from a balloon rubbing against her pussy. I move back to the action between her legs as the guy lets the balloon deflate against her clit then blows it up again.

I move on.

With every climax in the music, someone in the group has an orgasm.

I find Gil and Runa on a yellow airship. She's lying face down, straddling the balloon. Gil spanks her softly then slips his fingers inside her panties. Every time Bjork whispers, "Shhh," Gil kisses Runa's back. As the song crescendos, so does Runa. Gil pulls her underwear down, exposing her perfect milky white ass. He looks right at me, and we lock eyes through the camera as he fucks her. The music is blaring, Bjork is screaming. Gil keeps pounding. Runa comes.

Fade to black.

Gil walks me back to the car at four in the morning.

"Call me anytime you need a cameraman." I hold out my hand.

He shakes it and looks into my mouth. "You have great teeth."

I quickly purse my lips. This guy is into some kinky shit; who knows what he wants to do with my teeth.

"I'm an orthodontist, and I'm always looking for good teeth models. I can use you." He pulls out a card with his name and practice information.

"But you didn't do my teeth." Dad sent me to the dental school because it was cheaper than an actual dentist.

"So?" He shrugs. "Since when is advertising honest? I pay good money to my models. Give me a call next month—we're running a new ad campaign for fall."

I think of where I'll be in the fall. "Sounds good. I can always use the extra money."

Runa walks out of the warehouse in a long black coat and high-heeled boots. "Darling, I'm tired," she calls to her husband.

"Have a good night, Giovanni." Gil runs to her like a bitch. His arm slides around his wife's waist—her tiny, sexy waist.

Marriage wouldn't be so bad if you get to fuck a woman like for the rest of your life. Most nights I leave a job and return to my empty apartment. Not tonight. I drive home excited to have someone waiting for me.

***

My apartment smells like burnt coffee. Three mugs sit on the counter, along with a bowl, and a poorly folded newspaper. The couch is empty, but Leeyan's shoes are sitting in front of the coffee table.

"Honey, I'm home." I roleplay like this isn't my messy apartment. Like Leeyan isn't my best friend's baby mama.

She comes out of the bedroom with a carton in her hand and a spoon in her mouth. "How was it?" Her speech is impeded by a mouthful of ice cream.

"Were you eating in my room?"

"Uh, no." She shows me the empty carton. "I was just cruising the apartment, getting the lay of the land while I enjoyed some of your delicious coconut milk ice cream."

She walks into the kitchen, tosses the empty container in the trash and drops the spoon in the sink.

"Oops." She pulls it out, rinses it, the places it inside the dishwasher. Looking up with a satisfied grin. "Did you have to fuck anyone?"

Leeyan's ability to jump from one moment to the next makes me dizzy. She's moved from eating my emergency ice cream stash to making small talk about my gig.

"No, I didn't fuck anyone."

"That's good, I guess."

I wonder if there's more to her questions than curiosity. A little jealousy, maybe.

I unzip my hoodie and hang it in the closet.

"You owe me a carton of ice cream."

"Done." She skips ahead of me to the couch. "What did they hire you for? Did you dance?"

I sit and take off my shoes. "I filmed a fetish video."

She sits cross-legged on the couch, warming the air around me. She's intrigued and asks a million questions.

"It was a balloon fetish." I yawn and look at my watch. "Do you always eat ice cream at four-thirty in the morning?"

"I couldn't sleep so I stalked Theo online," she shrugs. "I also looked for apartments. My prospect fell through. So, I'm on to plan b."

'That's good. The apartment search, not the stalking," I chastise. "You could call him. Give him a heads up that you're coming back."

She shrugs again. "I don't know."

"If I let you hide out here, you have to agree to at least call him."

"I will." She does some kind of scout's honor gesture. "Is that it? No other house rules?"

"No walking around naked. In fact, no being naked period if I'm in the apartment. Shower when I'm gone." I get up and walk to the desk. "And stop dressing sexy."

She stands and looks down at her clothes.

"That sweater..."

"Is old and stained."

And you look hot as fuck in it.

"Burn it."

She holds up a finger as if a point is about to be made. "This can work—us as friends, roommates."

"Do we need a no sex rule?" I'm only half joking.

"I think we're on the same page when it comes to sex."

Did someone say sex?

Don't get excited—she means with other people.

"For the record, I don't want to see it, hear it, or smell it."

She scrunches up her nose. "Smell it?"

"Hey, I don't know what you're into."

She pulls her sweater off and spins it around her head before tossing it at me. It lands on top of my open laptop. She's wearing a black t-shirt underneath.

I give her a stern look. "You're already breaking the rules."

"You said take it off," she says defensively.

"I said burn it." I throw it back.

Is she intentionally trying to make me crazy or is she just being a brat?

Is there a difference? This friend thing is unfamiliar territory. Can you be turned on by a friend you're not allowed to fuck?

Yes. Hell yes.

"Did we not just have a talk about being sexy?"

"I'm being a good roommate." She tosses the sweater at me again.

"Is this a challenge?" I stand. "Because I will win."

The sexual tension built up from the looners gig paired with Leeyan's flirtatious behavior is a dangerous combination. There's only one way to relieve the situation. I pick up my phone and Bluetooth it to the audio system across the room. I open my music app and search the Bjork song. When the music begins, Leeyan falls backward onto the couch in hysterics.

I do a visual translation of the words in the song, dancing like I'm on Broadway, spinning like a fool. I pull my shirt off and rip the fly on my jeans open. Leeyan's jaw drops. Her eyes creep from my crotch to my eyes. I hold my finger to my lips, imitating the lyrics.

I twirl her around then pull her to me like we're ballroom dancing until my jeans slip halfway down my ass. Leeyan takes hold of my pants on both sides of my waist and pulls them up. Her fingers move swiftly over my fly; faster than it takes for blood to rush to my dick.

I grab her hands and lift them above her head. Then I freeze.

I don't know where to go from here.

I shouldn't even be here.

How the fuck did we get here?

"You're good." She's breathless like she's the one dancing.

The song ends, and I release her. "I win."

I walk to the desk and open my email.

"I have a rule," Leeyan finally says.

"You can't have rules."

"As a temporary occupant, I feel like I am entitled to certain regulations."

"Such as?"

"You can't walk around naked either—or shirtless." She tosses my shirt to me.

I grin, knowing I got to her. Being wanted is how I make a living. Leeyan isn't a job. She isn't a sexual prospect. She's a test, one I plan to ace.

CHAPTER EIGHT

The sidewalk outside Café DeLucci is busy with tourists. I watch them through Ray Bans while Rico works on his phone. We always sit outside—Rico likes to be on display. It isn't hot, but he's sporting a douche-fit: muscle shirt and shorts. He never passes up an opportunity to book a job. He's a walking advertisement for sex.

Face of a model.

Body of a god.

Tattoos of a biker.

The real star of his show is hidden inside his pants. They model dildos to look like Rico's dick. That monster launched his career. He posed nude for an art class and one of the students happened to run a talent agency. It was a run-of-the-mill strippers-for-hire setup, but after a few months, Rico quit his day job with a plumbing company and worked for her full time. Eventually, he bought the business. When Trance opened, he looked at the club as an opportunity to build his client list.

Not all the guys under Rico's employment fuck for money and not all of our clients want sex. I've been hired for more Christmas parties and company picnics than any other kind of date. When some of those dates end in sex, it's a bonus.

The server arrives with our food. He places a green salad in front of Rico, and a burger and fries in front of me. Rico lifts his fork as his eyes drop to my plate.

"You're slacking."

I pick up my cheeseburger and rip into it.

"Cheat day," I muffle. "I call it fatter-day."

He points his fork at me. "Good thing you aren't dancing tonight."

I'm missing another night at Trance for a side job. I'll have to kiss some serious ass to get Jim off my back, but I need the money.

I want to be ready to bail if shit goes south with Leeyan. Theo is in a good place, Leeyan can royally fuck him up. Unlike before, I won't be his shoulder to lean on. I'm the one tossing him a live grenade.

The grenade is in the East Bay today meeting someone about a job. She left a note on the refrigerator saying she'll be back tonight.

"You think Sway's up for a gig?" Rico cuts a cucumber in half with a knife and fork.

"Break him in with something easy like bachelorette party to see how he does in a more intimate environment." I take another bite of my burger, savoring every drop of grease, every morsel of meat.

"You're a fucking pig." Rico pokes at a tomato. "What about you—have you booked anything lately?"

Rico handles the jobs that come through his agency, but I handle my regulars and word-of-mouth gigs. Still, just because they book through me, it doesn't mean I keep all the money. I kick down ten percent to Rico. If it weren't for him, I wouldn't have clients in the first place. It's a courtesy.

"Nothing special." I lean back and rub my belly. "I have news about Brazil."

Rico sets his fork down. "Really?"

"She wants me settled by fall."

"And you're ready to do that?"

"I am."

"You have the funds?"

"Almost. If I give one hundred percent to the grind and stay out of the shops on Union Street, I'll be good."

Rico is against Brazil.

Well, it's more like he's against Antonia.

He thinks she's too good to be true, mainly because she always tries to negotiate a discount. Rico says heiresses aren't frugal.

Antonia likes to splurge, but she isn't willing to overpay for luxury.

"Look, bro, if you think this is a good move then you know I got you." He holds his fist out to me. "If you get down there and the club is a pit, there's no shame in coming home."

The thought has crossed my mind. Rio is flooded with bars that double as brothels. Antonia could be hiring me to manage an underground sex club, or worse, a sex trafficking ring. She has that female gangster aura about her.

I bump his fist. "My ticket isn't one-way—I'll be back to visit—but if this place is everything Antonia says it is..."

"What did she call it?" Rico interrupts. "The Studio 54 of Rio."

"She said people wait two hours to get in."

Rico looks skeptical. "And I bet they're doing coke by the pound and fucking in dark corners, too."

"That's every club," I reply defensively.

"You aren't running every club. You're managing the Studio 54 of Rio. So, when the cops raid this place—and you know they will—it's your ass going to jail." He pauses. "In Brazil."

"Food for thought," I concede.

"Dude, you don't need any more food today."

I burp and flip him off because he's right.

***

After lunch, I head home to shower and prep for my side job. The first thing I do is puke; the burger was too much. I flush the toilet and slather an obscene amount of toothpaste on my toothbrush. I scrub and rinse until I no longer feel like a fucking asshole. It isn't something I'm proud of, but it's my reality. Since Leeyan's been here, I've been slacking on my program. I haven't hit the gym in three days.

This side job is easy money, meaning no sex and no dancing. Rico offers a laundry list of services, including doing actual laundry, but today's gig requires a little more skill, which is why Percy is coming with me.

I meet him at the West Oakland BART station. He's already dressed for the gig in dark blue jean overalls, and the top part is folded down so you can see his plain white tee. A red and black flannel is tied around his waist to keep the overalls from sliding off his ass.

I shake my head as he gets into my car. "I can't believe you wore that on BART."

"You're wearing the same thing."

"Yeah, in my car." I pull away from the curb. "I could've picked you up."

"I stayed with my girl last night."

"Does Jim know you have a girlfriend?"

"It never came up." He shrugs. "Is it a problem?"

"Jim has a thing about girlfriends."

"What kind of thing?"

"He thinks they're bad for business."

If Jim finds out Percy is pussy-whipped, he may think twice about moving him up. He doesn't like to invest in dancers with short life spans.

"My girl's cool. She knows what I do."

So cocky.

So naive.

"Just keep it on the low. Don't lie if he asks, but I wouldn't volunteer the info."

"I got you." Percy holds his fist out to me.

The client's house is a renovated Victorian. Like most gentrified neighborhoods, the other homes haven't quite caught up to its level of sophistication. Across the street, a half-burned-out car houses a homeless man. He sets a can of tuna on the hood and opens a box of crackers. A calico cat runs out of the boarded-up house next door and waits by his feet.

I get out and pop open my trunk. Percy pulls out the red toolbox.

"Strap in." I pull the straps of my overalls over my shoulders and secure the buckles. Percy does the same. We look like gay farmers.

"I assume Rico gave you the rundown on what's going to happen in there."

"Yep, we're putting together some Ikea furniture."

"That's all he told you?"

"He said it was easy money." He shrugs like an arrogant punk.

Oh, this is going to be great.

I close the trunk. "Lead the way."

I want Percy to go in first—I want to see his face.

We walk up a red staircase to the porch. Percy doesn't react to the swing music vibrating the windows as he rings the doorbell.

The door opens and a flaming redhead screams, "They're here!"

He ushers us into the foyer, and his eyes drop to our feet.

"No shoes." He points to a hand-painted sign that says the same. "We have an assortment of slippers here, or you can go bare. The floors are sterilized weekly."

Several pairs of silk slippers are stacked in little wooden bins on the wall, organized by color. The foyer looks like the entrance to a preschool. Everything is pastel colored, from the walls to the flowers. I sit on the bench and remove my Timberlands, shoving my socks inside each one. I tuck my boots into the cubby beneath me.

"I'm Autumn." The client holds his hand out.

"Giovanni." We shake hands—it's part of the ritual. I've been here before with Dain.

Autumn turns to Percy, whose current facial expression is priceless. "You're a quiet one."

Percy doesn't acknowledge Autumn, still in shock.

"This is Percy." I backhand his arm. "Shoes, dude."

Percy peels his eyes from the main room where a dozen men dressed in bright pastel pants and matching shirts sip tea around several cardboard boxes.

Autumn hands me the fifteen-hundred-dollar fee, in cash, then asks if we'd like a drink. I tell him water is fine. When he disappears into the kitchen, I slap Percy on the head.

"Dude, focus."

He places his Converse into a cubby and puts on a pair of black satin slippers.

"We're supposed to be removing clothes, not adding them." I point to his feet. "Put those back. The floor is sterilized once a week—you can lick ice cream off this floor." I tap the hardwood with my foot.

He takes the slippers off. "I thought we were putting together furniture..."

"We are."

Autumn returns with two bottles of Voss. "Shall we begin?"

I take the water and remind Autumn of our no cell phone policy.

"All phones need to be collected. No photos, no video while we work. We can take pictures after." I tap Percy on the back. "Is that cool with you?"

"Uh, yeah...whatever."

Percy has no clue what I just said, too focused on our audience.

The first time I did a gig like this, I felt the same way. It's intimidating as fuck. I'll take the stage in front of a hundred people over a room of ten any day.

"Already collected." Autumn picks up a basket filled with cell phones.

"All right let's get started."

The room quiets when we walk in. They speak in low voices as we unpack the boxes and spread the pieces on the floor. Percy is like a robot. He moves only when I prompt him. We remove a large panel from the box and carry it to the hall, so it isn't in our way.

"What is going on here?" Percy is confused.

"They're going to watch us put this desk together."

"That's it? Just watch?"

"They do what they do, we do what we do. There's no contact."

He seems to settle down.

"Let's get this done and get out of here." Percy holds his fist out, and I bump it with my free hand.

This kid and his fist-bumping. Some of the viewers react to our show of bro-hood, mocking us with dainty fist bumps to each other. It's funny. Even Percy cracks a smile.

We have the two legs of the desk secured when the first request is made.

"Take your shirt off," a spectator calls out.

Percy shoots me a look. I look past him to the man holding the money. He has a one-hundred-dollar bill in each hand.

I stand and unhook the buckle on my right shoulder. The crowd whistles, and Percy follows my lead.

I pull my t-shirt off, and the room collectively sighs. This isn't like stripping on stage; it's strange to undress and get a mild reaction.

Percy takes his t-shirt off and tosses it at the man holding the money. The guy snatches it from the floor and sniffs it dramatically.

"He smells like a man."

"I want a sniff." Autumn reaches for the shirt, but the man pulls back.

"Get your own." He shoves Percy's shirt into a man purse by his blue satin-slippered feet.

Autumn pulls out another hundred. "Give it up, Giovanni."

I pick up my shirt and walk it to Autumn. You always treat the host with respect. I kneel in front of him and present the garment like a peasant making an offering to a king.

"Be still my heart," Autumn gushes. He takes the shirt then plants a kiss on my cheek.

"How much for the overalls?" A man wearing a bright yellow suit digs into his pocket and pulls out a wad of cash.

I never set a price. You should always let the client make an offer, but Percy didn't get this memo.

"Three fifty," Percy chirps.

The room lets out a chorus of "Ohhh."

"Do we have a bidding war?"

Big Yellow sits on the edge of his seat. "One fifty."

"Three hundred."

"One seventy-five."

They volley like this for a few minutes, and then Autumn intervenes when Percy moves to ten-dollar denominations.

"Let's call it a draw and meet halfway, shall we?"

He looks to me for approval. I pat Percy's shoulder to let him know it's time to concede.

"Two fifty it is," Autumn declares.

I pull the red flannel from my waist and let the overalls slide to my ankles. Again, the room quietly enjoys the view...until Percy drops his pants.

Even I laugh.

"Dude, what the fuck are those?"

"I didn't know we were stripping, okay?" He kicks his feet out of his overalls and adjusts his junk.

"Does Thor know you're wearing his underwear?"

"They were a gift from my girl. She knows I like Marvel." His face is almost as red as Thor's cape. "Don't fucking tell the guys, please."

"Is that a hammer in your pants or you just happy to see me?" Big Yellow laughs.

Percy looks like he wants to beat the old dude with a hammer.

Now that we're down to our underwear, every movement causes a stir from the audience. They focus on specific areas. When I bend over to screw the casters into the legs, I feel eyes burning into my ass. When I'm lying flat on my back, placing brackets under the desk, I know they're staring on my crotch. I can't help but feel like I'm being judged. Then comes the doubt.

Is my dick positioned weird?

Are my balls showing?

I should've shaved my inner thighs this morning.

Percy is putting the drawers together while I secure the top to the legs. Autumn walks into the room with a bowl of cherries and places it on the ground near the toolbox.

"Eat one," he instructs.

Percy sets his screwdriver down and turns to face the bowl. He's sitting on the floor with one knee up, legs spread open. I'd say he's pretty fucking relaxed now.

"I don't like cherries," Percy says defiantly.

Autumn lays a five-dollar bill on the floor and places two cherries on top. Percy grabs the cherries and the money. He eats them at the same time then spits the pits back in the bowl.

The brash, almost rude way he expels them from his mouth causes stir among the spectators, specifically Autumn, who continues to place cherries on top money.

Percy continues to eat the fruit.

I keep building the desk.

Once it's finished, we can leave, and that won't happen if Percy doesn't build the drawers. When Autumn places another round of cherries on a ten-dollar bill, I intercept.

"How about I get in on the action and you get back to work."

Percy reluctantly goes back to furniture assembly as I start eating cherries.

Sixty dollars later, he finishes, and I'm going to puke.

"Bravo." Autumn starts a round of applause.

"Where do you want it?" Percy asks.

Autumn laughs. "Oh darling, it doesn't exactly go with the décor."

"Then why did we put it together?"

Autumn looks perplexed. "Entertainment."

Percy is a smart kid, but sometimes he's really dumb.

"Thank you all so much for the hospitality." I pick up my overalls and the toolbox. Percy has one leg in his overalls as I push him toward the foyer. "Enjoy the rest of your evening."

I give him a warning glance as we strap into our overalls. He doesn't speak again until we're in my car on the freeway.

"What the fuck kind of freaky shit was that?"

"That was easy money, son."

I'll be shitting cherries for the next two days, but it was well worth the eleven hundred dollars in my pocket.

CHAPTER NINE

You have to be a special kind of friend to help another man with his erection. Teaching Theo how to tie off his dick before a private dance should earn me major friend points. It's the least I can do since I'm harboring his ex.

I'm doing reps on the pull-up bar when Percy walks into the locker room with a fresh stack of towels. He sets them on the shelf above the dirty bin and starts collecting the used ones from the floor.

"Good work at that side gig."

"Thanks, man. I appreciate the extra money." He pauses and looks around; we're the only ones in the room. "My girl thinks she's pregnant."

"Sorry, bro."

"Nah, it's happy news." He laughs. "We've been together for six months. Now that I'm making money, I can afford to put a ring on it." He smiles like that's something to smile about.

"I think Lowe's is hiring."

"Nah, man. I told you she's cool."

I wish him the best when his "cool" pregnant girlfriend forces him to quit.

Theo opens the bathroom door and I drop from the pull-up bar.

"Solid." I nod to his junk. "Now get your ass in there before your dick falls off."

I feel like a proud parent. I've been watching out for Theo since elementary school. His mom was a drunk. She'd go on a bender and leave him for days. The summers were the worst. I'd invite him over for dinner as often as I could, or until dad starting complaining about feeding strays.

The only time we haven't been one hundred with each other was after he started dating Leeyan. I said some pretty bad things about her before and after she came up pregnant. I accused Leeyan of trapping him. That's what chicks do—women trap men with magical pussy and surprise babies. Theo always saw the good in Leeyan—even after she left. He never stopped believing in her. I was the one who pushed him to move on. I felt justified in my perception of her. Until now. After hearing her side, I'll admit, Theo was right. Leeyan is a good person who made a bad decision. Life isn't judged on a single error. Leeyan still has a chance to knock it out of the park. I want to help her make it right. Not just for her, for Theo, too.

***

The gym isn't crowded at this hour. Just after lunch is my favorite time to work out. The mom classes are over, and the muscle heads are done for the day. It's only Theo and me. Like old times.

I help Theo lift the bar from the rack. "You doing ten?"

He takes the bar containing a measly hundred and forty pounds, and powers through the first five.

"You got this." I encourage him through the rest of this set. The boy can dance, but he can't lift for shit. I give him a little grief about his dad bod.

"Maybe I don't want to look like you," he lies.

I start to brag about how my body has created opportunities for me. I'm working up the nerve to tell him about Brazil. We've always had each other's backs. When I move, he'll be on his own. Even if he doesn't want Leeyan back, he'll have someone to help with Lulu. I could broker a truce between them and come out of this thing a hero. Two birds with one stone.

Before I find the right way to start the conversation, some creep rolls up on us. Theo's ignorant ass starts a conversation with him.

"I'm Josh," the creep says.

Theo shakes his hand. "Theo, and that's Giovanni."

Fucking hell.

Creepy Josh tries to talk to me, and I shut him down.

"Are you guys military?"

I slam my last rep and sit up. "Nope."

Theo doesn't realize Josh wants to use his dick as a toothbrush. The guy is seconds away from humping my leg. I remove myself from the situation and let Theo learn a valuable life lesson.

"Hey Gio," Sarah the receptionist leans over the counter to show me her tits. She's desperate and broke, but everyone is a potential client.

"Hey, sweetheart." I kiss her cheek. "You look good."

She blushes and asks about Theo. "Who's your friend."

"Ouch." I pretend to take on in the gut.

"Sorry." She runs her hand down my arm. "He looks more my type."

"What type is that?"

"Monogamous."

She must know I banged the receptionist who works nights and two of the personal trainers. I'm a Fitness Palace legend.

Theo finally breaks loose from Creepy Josh, and I introduce him to Sarah. While they make small talk, I hear my phone ding. I swipe the home screen and see a text from Leeyan. This feels wrong. I can't stand in front of Theo and text Leeyan.

Theo recognizes the nervous look I'm sporting as we walk to the locker room. Making a sexist remark is a great conversation changer. It also buys me time to get my shit together.

"She was so down she was practically on her knees." Referring to Sarah.

Theo denies it and launches into a tirade about being a daddy and some bullshit about respecting women. All I can think about is the message waiting for me from the only woman he's ever loved.

"I gotta bounce." Theo holds his fist to me.

"Yeah, give Lulu a hug for me." I set my phone down and get another ding. I feel like I should say something. He needs to be mentally prepared for her come back. When the shit hits the fan, I want to look back and know I tried to give him a heads up.

"Have you heard from Leeyan?"

Theo looks at me crazy. "Not in months. Why?"

I'm avoiding eye contact, so I don't give anything away.

"Nothing really, I just heard something." *What the fuck would you hear about Leeyan?* "You know that dude Andrew, owns the dry cleaners where she used to work?" *Good one.*

"Yeah. He's like forty-five and still lives with his mother."

"I was picking up some shirts, and he mentioned something about her coming home." I move my shower stuff around.

Theo says Leeyan hated the guy and would never reach out to him.

"Yeah, it's probably bullshit. That guy is a fucking wanker." I toss my towel over my shoulder and move towards the showers.

Theo leaves and I bang my head on the lockers. Man, that was harder than I thought it was going to be. I wait until I'm sure Theo has left the building before reading the message.

Leeyan: Staying with a friend. You're an only child...for the night.

Me: Anyone I know?

Even in text form that sounds desperate.

Leeyan: A friend from Germany.
Leeyan: A female friend.

That doesn't make me feel any better.

Me: You can always invite her back to the apartment for a sleepover? We can do each other's hair.

She sends back a crying/laughing emoji.

Leeyan: Don't worry, she's not that kind of friend.

Me: Who said anything about being worried?

Leeyan: ;)
Leeyan: I'll text you later. I left a surprise for you in the freezer.

I play it cool and don't reply back. When I get home, I go straight to the freezer and find two cartons of So Delicious coconut milk chocolate chip ice cream. I snap a picture and text it to her with a kissy face emoji. I instantly regret my emoji choice. Kissy face, really? A thumbs up would've been more appropriate. I consider texting one, then realize that would be weird. I'll wait until she texts back then decide.

Three minutes tick by and she hasn't replied back.

An hour later I'm glued to my desk.

With pizza.

I have a stack of prepped meals in the refrigerator, and I'm eating a large pepperoni pizza. It isn't gluten free.

I fold another slice into my mouth and chew it briefly before choking it down.

I'm not just waiting for Leeyan to reply to my message, Antonia is calling tonight. She's apartment hunting for me. Links to three places were in her last email. The one I forgot to reply to. At least I started my work permit and visa applications. I've also gotten through the basics in Rosetta Stone. I can say my name.

Alo, chamo-me, Giovanni

I can ask where the bathroom is, how much a bottle of wine costs— the important stuff. Antonia expects me to be conversation ready by the time I arrive. It took three years for me to learn how to order a burrito in Spanish, so her expectations are a little high.

I close the pizza box and take it to the kitchen. It's too large for my trash can, so I have to carry it to the garbage shoot at the end of the hall. It's the pizza box walk of shame.

I check the clock on the stove. Any minute, Antonia is going to call. My stomach turns in nervous anticipation—actually, that might be the pizza. I lean on the counter and take a few deep breaths. I think of the greasy pepperoni, the doughy crust, the cheese...so much cheese.

I run to the bathroom and vomit.

I've always been able to puke on demand. Vomiting to stay home from school was my go-to whenever I forgot to do my homework. Now I do it for other reasons. Kneeling on the cold tile floor, face first in the toilet is as vulnerable as I get. I'm not proud of vomiting my meals, but everyone has their demons.

I hear my computer ring, but I'm at the point where I can't stop. One last heave and I stand up. I grab a towel as I run to answer the call from Antonia.

I greet her in Portuguese. "*Olá. Como vão as coisas?*"

"*Bom trabalho!* Good job, Giovanni." Antonia is ecstatic. "I knew you wouldn't let me down."

I leave the computer to get a bottle of water and grab the Jameson instead. A shot of whiskey and a freshly empty stomach is not ideal, but fuck it.

"Did you look at the apartments?" She looks down at her phone. "The second one isn't available until September, but you can pay the down payment now and have it ready when you get here. What do you think?"

I take a shot and place the bottle on the desk. "I didn't look at it yet." I should've lied. I'm a liar; it's what I do.

"Gio," she whines. "Come on." Her pouty face used to be sexy, but now it's annoying. She doesn't look like my fuck buddy—she looks like my boss.

"I promise I will check it out after we hang up. If you say it's good, I trust you."

"Good, then send me the money and I'll put down the deposit for you." She's testing me. It's time to put up or shut up.

"You'll have the money tomorrow."

"That's what I want to hear." She looks over her computer screen as if someone has walked into her room. She's sitting at a desk with a large king-sized bed behind her, and whoever strolled in just put a *fuck me* smile on her face.

"I have to go, Gio. I'll start the paperwork for the apartment. I'm having your work visa taken care of."

126

She must be calling in a favor to push it through.

"Thank you, Antonia. I really appreciate all your help."

"Don't let me down, darling, *tchau.*"

Her call disconnects. I exhale.

I'm walking to the bathroom to brush my teeth when my phone buzzes. Fuck my breath. I pull my phone from the charger and find the text I've been waiting for.

Leeyan: Food porn. I love it.

Me: Anytime I read the word porn, I get an instant boner.

That was an overshare.

Leeyan: I'll remember that.

Me: What time will you be home?

Fuck. I shouldn't have wrote home. I should have said back. or when will you return. Home sounds too, homey.

Leeyan: Miss me already?

I choose my words wisely and decide to go with a lie.

Me: I might have a 'friend' over. Wouldn't want you to hear it, see it, or smell it.

It takes her four minutes to reply.

Leeyan: I'll surprise you. ;)
Leeyan: Have a good night.

She didn't fall for it, not even close. I'm an idiot.

CHAPTER TEN

Fred calls to let me know Leeyan is downstairs. I tell him to let her up. I've wasted the entire day waiting for her return. At least I didn't eat any ice cream. I sit at the desk and pretend to be busy.

"Honey, I'm home!" She sings as the door opens.

"What's up," I grunt.

She drops her backpack on the floor, kicks her shoes off, then plops on the couch. "I'm so hungry."

"There's ice cream."

She leans on the back of the couch, her face resting on the cushions as she watches me. "Did you eat lunch?"

I shake my head no as I click on the links Antonia sent. Clicking and intermittent typing gives the illusion that I'm busy.

"I have work to do." I motion to the computer. It's a lie but I need to focus my energy on something other than her.

"Did you fun last night?" She looks around the apartment.

If I lie again, it proves how weak I am. "I decided to just chill. How was your night?"

Leeyan grins. She knows my text was a lie and I don't care. Honestly, I want her to know I was alone.

"It was okay. We went to a Mexican restaurant and had a few pitchers of margaritas. Typical girl's night." She goes to the kitchen and returns with a bottle of water. "Are you learning to speak Portuguese?"

"How did you know?"

"I saw the Rosetta Stone app on your screen."

"Why were you on my computer?"

The last thing I need is Leeyan snooping around my laptop and accidentally accepting a video call from Antonia.

"I was checking Craigslist for apartments the other day." She walks back to the sofa.

"You can check Craigslist on your phone," I inform her.

My phone rings on the coffee table and Leeyan picks it up.

I dash around the desk, over the couch, and snatch the phone from her. "Do we need to have a talk about privacy?"

"Chill, dude. It's just your mom." She pretends it isn't a big deal.

"New rule: don't touch my technology."

"These hands will not go near your technology." She holds them up and wiggles her fingers. "Unless you want me to touch your technology."

"I don't."

"Never say never," she whispers.

I answer the call and flick my hand in her direction.

Leeyan decides to take the trash out. She picks up the pizza box and looks inside. She gives me a knowing smile.

"Don't forget that." I point to her sweater hanging on a hook near the door.

"I can't believe you're seriously making me throw this away."

"My house, my rules." I cringe as Leeyan walks out the door. I sound just like my old man.

Mom answers on the fifth ring.

"Hey Ma."

"*Patanino*," she greets me. "You're coming for dinner tonight?"

"I wasn't planning on it."

"It's your father's birthday, Giovanni. You have to come. He's only fifty once."

"I know how aging works, Ma."

Leeyan walks back inside and washes her hands in the kitchen sink.

"I'm making pistachio cake."

My favorite, not Dad's—it's a bribe to get me over there.

"Bring a friend. You know how much your father likes Theo, and I haven't seen Lulu since Christmas."

Mom loves Lulu, treats her like a grandchild, and Lulu may be the only one she ever has. I'm too selfish to have kids, like someone else I know. Leeyan turns the water off.

"He has to work tonight, and so do I."

My mother knows I work at Trance, but what I do there is somewhat of a mystery. I tell her I wait tables and greet guests. A quick internet search would provide her with the truth, but Maria Castillo isn't the kind of woman to google her son.

"He's your father, Giovanni. You should be here. We have things to discuss." Her tone isn't pleasant or demanding; she sounds desperate.

Leeyan is looking through all my cabinets as I debate about whether or not to blow off work. I really don't want to see Theo and have to lie to his face. I also don't want to leave Leeyan's nosy ass alone in my apartment.

"Okay, Ma. I'll be there, and I'm bringing a friend."

***

"Are you sure this is a good idea?" Leeyan fans herself with the birthday card I picked up at the corner store. "Can you make this any colder?" She fidgets with the air conditioning.

"Can you not touch my car?" I slap her hand away. "Roll the window down—it's colder outside."

The fog has rolled in and blanketed my parents' neighborhood in a soggy mist.

"Do your parents know about me?"

"You mean do they know about you ditching Lulu when she was two?"

"Why is it when a woman joins the army she's ditching her family, yet a man joins and he's a hero?"

"Cause life sucks." I roll the windows up because I'm freezing. "And yes, they know, but we don't have to tell them who you are. I'll just say you're a friend."

"That'll work?"

"My parents won't ask a lot of questions."

It only takes two loops around the block to find parking. Leeyan is holding the bottle of red wine and the birthday card. Maybe the old man will enjoy it more if he thinks she picked it out.

"You grew up in the Aves, huh?" Leeyan takes a dig at me.

The Avenues are part of San Francisco, but living out here is like a suburb of the city.

"Sorry I'm not cool like you. I didn't have junkie parents."

"Whoa, dude. I'm just fucking with you."

"Sorry, this neighborhood brings out the cocksucker in me."

We turn the corner onto my block and the first thing I see is the big red and white *SOLD* sticker on the sign under my tree.

Leeyan sees it too. "Your parents are moving?"

This is bad—really bad.

Across the street is Josie's house. She doesn't live there anymore, but her daughter does. Our families have been friends for over twenty years, and they wouldn't just kick my parents out—*would they?*

"Wait here," I tell Leeyan.

I ring the bell, not really sure what I'm going to say. Getting angry won't help. I'm only here for information, that's it.

The door opens, and a redhead appears. Her hair is in a knot on top of her head, small tendrils framing her face—the face of my childhood. We learned to ride bikes together, watched scary movies under the covers at my house. At one point in my life, we were best friends.

"Giovanni?" She looks me up and down. "Oh my god, it's so good to see you!" She steps onto the porch to give me a hug.

"Hey Mags, you look good."

She pulls away. "What are you doing here?" She looks past me to the street, where Leeyan is shivering in the mist. "Is she with you?"

"Uh, yeah. She's a fri...she's my roommate."

Mags laughs. She isn't buying it. Before Theo came along, I spent all my waking hours with Maggie. One day I dared her to kiss me and she did. After we kissed, she changed—started wearing makeup and giggling at my stupid jokes instead of calling me a dickwad. She's the reason I don't have female friends. Kissing ruined our friendship.

"One of my sorority sisters had her bachelorette party at Trance."

"You were at the club? Why didn't you say hi?"

Thank god she didn't.

"Cause it's hella awkward seeing your junk bounce around in a G-string. Plus, we were in the private room. They wouldn't let us go back and forth to the main room."

"It's a crowd control thing," I explain. "The club only holds so many in the main room."

"You didn't knock on my door to discuss fire codes."

Maggie is always to the point.

"The house sold?" I shrug like *What the fuck?*

"It's under contract, but my mom thinks the buyers are going to pull out after the inspection. She got a report on the roof and the electrical. It all needs to be updated, and they won't be able to move in until everything is fixed."

"But it's okay for my parents to live there?"

"My mom offered to update the house. They refused to move out, even temporarily."

134

My immigrant parents have a fear of moving. I'll never understand how people can leave their country for America. Once here, they refuse to move to another neighborhood, even if it's a better place.

"Where are my parents supposed to go when the house eventually sells?" I'm getting heated. I can't help it.

"They know the situation. My mom gave them first dibs on the property, but they didn't want it."

"They can't afford it!" I snap. "What the fuck, Mags? Your family has enough money. Why can't they just let them stay until..."

"Until they die, Gio? This isn't about money. Mom is retiring. She wants to sell and move somewhere quiet. Sorry if that's inconvenient to you." She starts to slam the door in my face.

"Maggie." I catch the door. "I'm sorry. You guys have done a lot for them. I appreciate it."

"Alberto and Maria are family to me, to all of us. Mom wouldn't sell if she thought it would hurt them." Maggie places her hand over mine. "Take care, Gio."

I return to Leeyan and we cross the street.

"I like redheads." She jabs me in the side with her elbow.

"She was the first girl I ever kissed."

"I knew she was an ex!" Leeyan socks me in the arm. "She had that look in her eyes."

"What look?"

"Like she was debating on whether or not she should slam the door in your face or pull you inside and hate-bang you."

135

Leeyan is right. If I wanted to, I could have Mags. She came with too many strings. When I eventually broke her heart; it would affect both our families. Who wants that kind of guilt on their conscience?

I open the front door without knocking, something I haven't done in years. "Ma!" I yell, just like I did when I was a kid.

"*Patanino!*" she calls from the kitchen.

I step into the living room and see my father's balding head resting against the back of his chair.

"Happy Birthday, Pop."

He looks back at me and grunts.

"This is my friend, Lee." I look at her like *Just go with it.*

When he sees her beside me, he jumps up.

"Hello." He coughs into his fist. "Sorry, I have a little cold."

Leeyan extends her hand. "Happy Birthday, Mr. Castillo."

He shakes her hand. "Call me Al."

"This is for you." She gives him the wine and the card.

He looks at the label with an impressed expression.

"I'll open it now, so it can breathe." He walks to the kitchen, yelling for the wine opener.

"I brought that same bottle over on Christmas. He said it was too bitter."

"It's all about presentation," Leeyan whispers.

Dad returns with the open bottle and gestures for us to sit at the dining room table. I take my seat, and Leeyan sits between my father and me.

"Should we taste it?" I suggest.

136

Dad pours us each a glass. He takes the first sip. "Oh, this is good." He points at Leeyan. "She has good taste in wine."

Even if he doesn't know I chose the wine, having him say he likes it is enough. Leeyan doesn't seem to think so.

"Actually, Giovanni picked this bottle." She squeezes my arm.

Dad chokes mid-sip. "Really?" He clears his throat. "Well you must have been a good influence on him. Usually his taste in wine is shit."

"Okay," Mom says from the door. "Who is your friend?"

Leeyan stands, and I follow her lead.

"Mom, this is Lee." I place my hand on the small of Leeyan's back. It's a natural movement, one I don't realize I've made until she looks at me. The gesture is one of protection, but who is protecting whom?

"Pink, huh." Mom doesn't know what to make of Leeyan's short colorful hair. "It's pretty."

"Pretty in pink," I joke.

Nobody gets my reference, not even Leeyan.

I sit back down. "I'm starving."

The spread my mother prepared is enough for ten people, maybe fifteen. We grunt through small talk as we eat. Mom asks a lot of questions about how we know each other, where we met, how long we've been dating.

"We're friends, Ma," I tell her for the sixth time.

"*We're friends*," she mocks. "But what does that mean these days? Nobody wants to commit. Everyone is friends. Can you marry your friend?"

"If I found the right person, someone I considered a friend...if I loved that person, I would get married." Leeyan is careful not to drop any pronouns because she isn't committed to one sex.

"Gio has never brought a girl home." Mom looks at me with a knowing expression. "That means something. I don't know what, but it's something."

Leeyan stifles a laugh. I choke on a ravioli.

"You never said what you do for a living." Dad finishes the rest of the wine. "Do you, um, work with our son?"

"No," Leeyan replies in horror—a little too much horror.

Dad smiles in relief. "Good, that's good."

She's good and I'm bad. Little does he know.

"She just got out of the army," I blab.

Leeyan kicks me under the table. My parents aren't that dense. They can put two and two together, especially Mom. She knows Theo's ex is in the military. I swear I see a light bulb dangle above Mom's head. She looks at Leeyan as if she's looking for something. I follow her eyes to a frame on the sideboard. It's a photo of Lulu.

I need to keep Mom off Leeyan's scent.

"Are we going to talk about the sold sticker on the sign in front of the house?"

Dad waves his hand in the air. "Don't worry about it. The buyers are going to change their mind."

"Even if they do, the house is going to sell at some point. Do you have a plan?"

Leeyan pats my thigh to calm me down, which riles me up in another way. I shove her hand away. She pushes me back.

I look up and find Mom watching us.

I place both of my hands on the table. "Maggie seems to think you guys are okay with them selling the house."

"We have faith, Gio. Don't you worry." Mom points at me like I'm in trouble. She's the one on the verge of losing her home because of poor financial planning and I'm being scolded.

"Whatever you need, I'm sure Giovanni will support you." Leeyan smiles at my mom. She has no clue the can of worms she just popped open.

"Giovanni will support us?" Dad snarls. "With what, his dancing money?"

Leeyan's mouth falls open. "I meant..."

This time I place my hand on her leg. She shrinks into the chair.

"We don't need his help. We do fine on our own. He does fine on his own. Nobody bothers anybody. He likes it that way." Dad shoves his plate away as if the conversation has made him lose his appetite.

Just when I think things can't get any worse, Leeyan opens her mouth again. "Your son is a very generous, caring, selfless person."

Oh sweet Jesus, let her choke on a meatball.

"My son only cares about things—cars, clothes, and fancy shoes." Dad pushes away from the table to stand.

"I'm sorry, Mr. Castillo, but you're wrong. Giovanni puts the needs of others in front of his own every day. The people he meets never forget his kindness, how he made them feel. Only a special human can make a broken, lonely person feel hopeful again."

My father isn't the only person at the table with his mouth hanging open. I'm right there with him.

"I know my son is a good man," Mom adds. "Maybe too good sometimes." Her eyes narrow in contempt.

She figured it out.

"We should go." I finally stand. "Mom, thank you for dinner." I lean down to kiss her cheek.

"What about cake?"

"Forget it..."

"I'd love some cake." Leeyan just won't stop.

Mom pushes away from the table. "I'll put it in a to-go." She leaves to pack up half a cake for me.

It's just Dad and me in the dining room when Leeyan excuses herself to use the bathroom.

"I like her," he finally says. "Bring her back."

"We'll see."

CHAPTER ELEVEN

I always drink half a bottle of whiskey after dinner with my parents. Tonight is no exception. I pull the new bottle of Jameson from the bag and grab two glasses from the cabinet.

"You want?" I hold the bottle up.

"I need." Even she's stressed after dinner with my parents. "Let me change first."

I sit on the sofa and check my phone. I have two missed calls from Jim and six texts from Theo. No-showing is a dick thing to do at the club, and missing tonight will set me back with the Jim. I'll be lucky if he lets me keep my spot in the rotation.

"Sorry, my dad is kind of a dick."

Leeyan joins me on the couch, having changed into the gray sweats and an army t-shirt. Her hair is clipped on the left side to keep it off her face. I like this stripped-down version of her.

She pours herself a glass and sits beside me. "What's his deal?"

"First off, I quit baseball."

She makes an *ouch* face. "That's my fault, right?"

Yes. "No."

"The trickle-down effect. Theo left school because I was pregnant and begged him to come home. You left a month later."

"I never wanted to be there in the first place. I only went to college because Theo needed me."

"We both made life-altering choices to please Theo." She shakes her head. "Except he didn't knock you up and force you to bail on your dreams."

"That's harsh."

"That's the truth. I didn't want to have a kid not at eighteen or even twenty-eight. I know there are women in the world who'd kill to have a baby. The difference between me and them–it's their choice."

"Technically, you had choices."

She looks at me like I'm clueless. "Louisa was Catholic. I let her down by getting pregnant at eighteen by a boy I barely knew. Having an abortion would've destroyed her."

Leeyan is visually emotional at the mention of Louisa. She passed away a year and a half ago of cancer. They didn't find it until it was too late, she only lived a few months after her diagnosis.

"I didn't come home for the funeral because I knew if I got on an airplane and flew back here, I'd never want to leave."

I tell her the service was nice. Dennis, Louisa's son, spared no expense.

"He inherited everything, so he has a lot to spare." Her bitter tone tells me all I need to know about her feelings for Dennis.

"Theo thinks Dennis is in love with you."

142

"Dennis is a spoiled brat. He only loves himself and money." She holds her glass to mine. "Sounds like someone else I know."

"I'm offended."

"No you're not." She lays her head on the back of the couch and looks up at me. Her lips are pink, smooth. I wonder what it feels like to kiss them.

"Hello?" She waves her hand in front of my face.

"What?"

"Were you just staring at my mouth?" She bites her lip.

"No." *Yes.*

"I think you were."

"I don't look at you like that."

"Like what?" She pretends to be offended.

"Like a woman." Now she really looks offended. "I mean, you know, like someone I'd fuck."

Fuck is harsh. I should have said *sleep with* or *hook up with* or *find attractive*. Everything sounds wrong.

Leeyan places her glass on the coffee table and sits cross-legged, facing me like she's about to get serious.

"So, I'm not fuckable?"

My palms sweat. "I don't know."

"You just said..."

"I said you aren't someone *I'd* fuck. I'm sure there are lots of dudes and chicks who would fuck you, just...you know, none that live here."

"To be clear: you would not fuck me?"

My face is red hot, my dick semi-hard.

"Absolutely not." I take a shot of whiskey.

Leeyan holds my gaze then picks up her glass. "Okay, you want to watch a movie?"

If that was a test, I fucking aced it.

I only have one television, and it's hanging on the wall in my bedroom. "I have a rule about drinking in bed."

"You have a lot of rules, Giovanni."

My name sounds good coming from her lips.

"Let me guess, you want to break them?"

She smiles with half her mouth at my somewhat flirtatious remark.

"I just spent three years in the army, so yeah, I guess you can say I'm ready to break a few rules."

An hour later Leeyan is dancing on the main floor of DV8. It's an old club in the city with a shitty sound system and crappy bartenders, but I know the DJ because he used to spin at Trance.

"She's fine." Tone admires Leeyan from the DJ booth. "How long you been hittin that?"

"She's strictly friend zone."

"What a waste." He takes a swig from his beer as he checks his laptop. Tone doesn't know Theo, so I feel like it's safe to be a little honest.

"She's my boy's ex. Serious baby-mama drama happening there."

Tone makes that face dudes make when you're playing with fire.

"Oh hell no! That isn't friend zone, bro. That's the danger zone."

I know.

I'm hit with a heavy dose of nostalgia as I watch Leeyan on the dancefloor. Her is hair stuck to her forehead, and the strap of her black tank top is sliding down her right shoulder. I imagine an alternate universe where she is mine. A world where she never met Theo, didn't join the army, and never had Lulu. As soon as I think it I know it's wrong. Theo and Leeyan may not be meant for each other but Lulu was destined to be born. If that means two wrong people end up together for a brief moment in time, then so be it.

Leeyan looks up at me with a smile and her fingers form the universal sign for drink.

"I'm gonna hit the bar."

"That ain't all you're hittin tonight." Tone shakes his head at me.

I shake his hand and pat his back before running downstairs before someone intercepts Leeyan. When I get there she already has a drink, courtesy of the bartender, and the girl from the dance floor is hanging on her side with another dude waiting to introduce himself. Leeyan is like a magnetic force, people are drawn to her. I'm one of them.

"Want to get out of here?" *There's way too much competition.*

She pounds her drink and takes my hand. "Let's go home!"

I like the way that sounds.

My apartment has always been a place of solitude, somewhere to store my clothes and sleep. As much money as I've invested in making it look like a place to live, it's never felt like home until now.

I suggest we walk a few blocks to cool off before booking an Uber. Really, I want to be outside with Leeyan. We spend most of our time cooped up inside. Afraid someone will see us.

"I miss this—walking for the sake of walking. Everything I've done for the last three years has been for a purpose. There's no wasted time. Every second counts."

"No days off," I chime in, quoting an inspirational meme I saw online.

"Exactly." She unravels the hoodie from her waist and slips it on. "I forgot how much fun it was to dance." She spins and loses her balance slightly.

I grab her forearm to guide her around a wet spot on the sidewalk, and she runs her hand down my arm until our palms are pressed together. Holding hands with Leeyan gives me a knot in my stomach, like I'm in eighth grade and secretly hanging out with my best friend's girl. It's becoming increasingly difficult to remember who she is, why she's here.

"Remember that shirt you used to wear all the time? The one with those fat rainbow bears." She wore it the night she met Theo.

"Care Bears!" she recalls. Her reply echoes down Fourth Street. "I loved that shirt."

"Lulu sleeps in it. Theo tied it up so it wouldn't fall off her."

She smiles with tears in her eyes. "It might not seem like it on the outside, but I miss her so much it hurts. I'm scared she's going to hate me. I'd rather keep pretending she thinks of me with a smile on her face than actually see her smile." She leans into my side, shivers softly. "That makes me the queen of assholes."

"We're all assholes."

"Not you, not really." She nudges me. "Look at everything you've done for me, and you hate me."

I don't correct her; I can't without divulging my feelings. "I have assholeness in me."

She stops walking. "Name one thing you've done that would make me stop and say, 'He's an asshole.'"

"I'm moving to another country, so I won't be here to see them tossed out on the street, eating out of garbage cans."

"You're really going to move to Brazil?"

This is the first time I've mentioned my move. I know she snoops, but we've never actually talked about it.

"Yes, it's a dream job."

"You're going to live your dream..."

"And my parents are going to be homeless."

"You still have time to do the right thing."

"Like what? I'm moving in a matter of months."

I feel her stiffen at the thought of me leaving. Leeyan is strong on the outside, but inside she's vulnerable and scared. Right now, I'm the reason she hasn't fallen apart. She needs me, even if she'll never admit it.

"Okay, well, maybe you can sublet your apartment to them."

I try to imagine my mother shopping at Whole Foods downtown. She still goes to the same neighborhood produce market and grocery store from my childhood. It sells more organic and gluten-free food now, but it's familiar.

"My parents hate change."

"Change for the sake of change isn't the same as change to survive. When those instincts kick in, they'll appreciate your offer."

I don't even know if I can sublet my place. I'm only in that building because Antonia pulled some strings. Also, there's no way my parents can afford the rent unless I find a way to help them—am I willing to do that?

My phone rings, and at this hour, it's most likely a job, one I should take but won't because I'm too involved with my houseguest.

"Who is it?" Leeyan tries to sneak a look as I pull my phone out.

"It's Antonia."

"Are you going to answer it?"

"No." I deny the call and shove my phone deep into my pocket.

She shrinks in my arms. "I'm totally fucking up your life." She hiccups. "If I wasn't here...if I had balls, I'd suck it up and go see them."

"You just need more time."

"Maybe too much time has passed. Lulu doesn't know me. I don't know her. I don't even know how she eats her oatmeal. Does she like raisins or blueberries? Does Theo let her add extra brown sugar? Does she prefer Cream of Wheat?"

I laugh even though she's not trying to be funny.

"That's the kind of thing I thought about when I was in Germany. Trivial things like can she read, is she potty-trained. Even though the answers were a phone call away,

I felt like I didn't deserve to know, like I lost the right to care because I left."

We stop walking and I take her by the shoulders. "You have every right to miss Lulu. She is your daughter no matter where you are."

Her eyes are blurry. "The rules aren't the same for women. I saw it firsthand. Women on base were constantly questioned about the kids they left behind, how their husband feels about having a wife in the military. Never once did I witness a man getting grilled for leaving his family."

She's right. If the tables were turned, nobody would see Theo as a selfish prick for wanting to serve and protect. Even I'm guilty of this behavior. Nobody was as harsh to Leeyan as me.

"I'm sorry. I had no right judge you, to say all those nasty things the day you left."

"It's okay, you were protecting Theo. Honestly, I knew he'd be fine without me because he had you. We didn't see eye-to-eye on a lot of things but when it came to Theo, we were always on the same page. I never set out to hurt him. I was just trying to save myself."

I kiss her on the forehead. There's nothing friendly about the way my lips linger against her salty skin.

She leans in closer. "I'm scared, Gio."

"Scared of what?"

"Of this. I should want to see my daughter more than I want to be here with you."

Her words cause a stir, and not just in my pants.

"You've done so much for me. I wish I could..."

She stops midsentence and closes her eyes. I wait a few seconds, hoping she'll finish. Instead, she rests her head against my chest. We stand on the empty street, holding each other in the dark. People hurry past, determined not to ruin our moment. It's common courtesy among nightcrawlers.

The city is an entirely different place at night—no suits walking with purpose to their next appointment or tourists snapping pictures of sights we take for granted. In the early morning hours, when mist from the unrelenting fog settles over the streets, we reclaim the city. Darkness is our time. On this dark street in the middle of downtown, I slip a hand under my wall and pull Leeyan in. I feel her in every way someone can feel another human. Everything until now has been blurred—my feelings, her intentions. Holding Leeyan in my arms, I know one thing for sure—it's going to hurt like hell when she leaves.

CHAPTER TWELVE

I've spent the last week working as much as I can. I need to make up the funds I lost by missing shifts at Trance. Rico booked us in a fashion show in Los Angeles; the pay was shit, but I boosted a Gucci sports coat I can sell on Poshmark or eBay, and it's already brought me good luck—the CEO I saw last night commented on the coat during my flight home. I gave her a card, and three days later she was on all fours in a suite at the Fairmont calling me daddy. Even though the woman was beautiful and sexy, and rich—the sex wasn't pleasurable. My dick wouldn't have worked if it wasn't for Viagra. The money isn't the only reason I've taken every job Rico has thrown at me. I'm avoiding Leeyan.

I slip into the apartment at dawn. Leeyan is sleeping on the sofa, her bare leg visible from the doorway. I want to be the guy who doesn't look, but I do—every chance I get. She stirs, and I jerk my eyes away.

Leeyan has invaded every aspect of my life. I think about her when I'm with other women, wonder what she's wearing, eating. This whirlwind friendship can only end in heartache. There's a fifty-fifty chance it's my heart that will break. Leeyan's confession the other night spooked both of us. She's been aloof, even more than me. We've dumbed down our interactions to basic roommate chit-chat.

I walk past the kitchen counter and find a mess of another kind: a dirty plate, three containers from the Chinese restaurant on the corner, and an empty bag of Oreos. Leeyan isn't even pretending to be a good houseguest anymore. The more I stay away, the messier she becomes, but if this kitchen is the only mess I have to deal with, so be it. It's a miracle I've been able to keep this from Theo for as long as I have. Avoiding him at Trance isn't easy, but he's been distracted too. I hope he's prepared for the bomb about to land on his doorstep.

Fruit-scented shampoo bottles clutter the floor of my shower. They're the kind you get on sale at Target, two for five dollars—cheap. I don't like cheap. I don't like pink razors on my sink or wet towels on my leather couch. My apartment is in disarray.

Not much longer, I whisper to myself.

I emailed Antonia to assure her I'm still on track. Brazil is my exit plan. When shit goes south with Theo after he finds out about Leeyan, I'm out of here.

In the middle of my shower, Leeyan knocks on the door.

"Yeah," I reply.

"Just wanted to make sure it was you and not some psychopath who likes to shower before raping and murdering."

"You were in the army—weren't you trained in hand-to-hand combat?" My hand slips below my waist. Washing my dick while talking to Leeyan feels wrong, which is why it feels good. "I bet you're pretty good with a gun."

"Guns were my least favorite thing about the army."

That makes no sense. "What did you dislike about them?" I want to keep her talking as I slather more body wash into my hand. "Cleaning them?"

"Shooting them. Guns kill. I'm not a killer."

I stop washing. "I thought the army was your dream job. Being all you can be and all that."

"The army was an escape from my reality."

Honesty is a boner-killer.

I rinse the soap off. "And now you're back in reality."

"Sort of." Her voice trails off.

"Hey, let's finish this conversation when I'm not naked."

"Good idea. I'll make coffee."

I get out of the shower, dress, and meet her in the kitchen.

My apartment is warm because my houseguest is always cold. I check the thermostat and adjust the temp to a less tropical climate. Leeyan is sitting on the counter next to the glass cooktop I haven't used in two weeks.

"There's a gym on the second floor—go work out, generate some body heat, sweat."

"Gyms are for pussies. I like to run." She scoops a spoonful of cereal into her mouth and turns the page on the latest issue of Maxim.

"Then go run."

"Maybe later." She slurps another spoonful of milk.

"How's the apartment search going?" I pour the last of the cereal into a bowl. "Jesus Christ, I bought this yesterday." I toss the box onto the pile making its way up the wall.

"You have good taste in cereal."

"I have good taste in everything." *Except roommates.*

Leeyan hops down and places her bowl in the dishwasher without rinsing it first. I want to say something, but I can't without sounding like a bitch.

"I decided to go with my last resort," she says regarding her living situation.

"The Green Tortoise wasn't the last resort?"

"Not even close."

"Do I want to know the details?"

"The place isn't the issue, it's who owns it."

Where she lives shouldn't be my concern.

Leeyan Flores isn't my problem.

"Have you given any more thought to how you plan to tell Theo you're home?" I finish my cereal and rinse my bowl.

She fidgets with the string on her sweats. "I thought I'd just show up on his doorstep."

"Yeah, 'cause surprises like that always go well." I place my bowl in the dishwasher, which is full enough for a cycle.

I could go a week without accumulating this many dishes. Leeyan, however, seems to go through bowls, plates, and cups like she's been feeding an entire platoon. What she does here when I'm out vexes me.

The other night Leeyan sent me a text during a dinner date. My client had just asked me to her room for a nightcap when my phone dinged. It was my bad—I forgot to turn off the ringer. Any other day, I would've ignored it, but it isn't every day I have a woman stashed in my apartment. When my date excused herself to use the ladies' room, I pulled up the text with all the giddiness of a fifteen-year-old girl. It was a picture of a banana wearing an American flag G-string. The caption: *Your laundry was delivered.* She thought it was hilarious until I told her Theo had the same one.

I was so engrossed in my conversation with Leeyan, I didn't realize the client had returned. She decided watching me text was a turn-off, and I lost at least two grand when she cut the date short.

"I have to get ready." I place my hand on her shoulder as I walk past. I don't know why I do this. Touching her is wrong, yet I find myself doing it every chance I get.

"Will you see Theo tonight?"

"No, he has the night off." I walk into the bedroom and pull my gym clothes from their drawer. Theo is going on his first side job.

I return to the kitchen where Leeyan is putting two pieces of my organic wheat bread into the toaster.

"My cereal wasn't enough?"

"I had a small bowl." There's no shame in her game.

"I only have peanut butter."

"Peanut butter is my fave." She pulls a knife from the drawer then knocks it closed with her hip.

The old me could never have had a woman in the apartment like this—casual, platonic. I admit there are times I imagine what it would feel like to bend her over the couch and fuck her into next week—I am a man—but mostly she annoys me, even more so now that we have a no whiskey rule.

"Please wash the knife in the sink—peanut butter never comes off in the dishwasher."

"Yes, sir!" She salutes.

I walk around the counter to the bench by the door and grab my gym bag. "I won't be too late tonight. You want to me pick up some food?"

The toast pops up and Leeyan removes them from the toaster.

"No, I'm out of here."

My bag drops to the floor with a thud. "Really?"

She looks up with a sad expression hidden behind the fake it til you make it smile. "Don't worry, I'll clean before I go. It'll be like I was never here."

If only that were true. My apartment will never be the same, will never feel the same. "So, you're ready to see Lulu and Theo?"

"I finally grew some balls, big hairy ones."

"Thanks for that visual."

She places the knife in the sink. "I can't pay you back for everything you've done."

"Please, don't even—"

"Let me say this, okay?" Her hands are flat against the marble counter like it's holding her up, supporting her. "I lost everything when I left—friends, respect, love...so many things. I spent three years pretending I didn't need anyone. It's a shitty way to live, especially when I had people here who missed me." She walks around the counter and gives me hug. "Thank you for giving me time, Gio. I wouldn't be ready to see my daughter if it wasn't for you."

I don't feel like I've done anything to earn her praise, but sometimes it isn't about you; it's how others perceive your actions.

"I'm going to see Lulu tonight," she gushes.

"She's going to love you." *Who wouldn't?*

"And Theo? Do you think he's going to forgive me?"

He'd be a fool not to.

***

After the gym, I meet Rico for lunch at our usual spot.

"Tell me about Theo's gig." I stab a crouton with my fork and savor the carbs. It's salad day since I'm dancing tonight and haven't meal prepped since Leeyan's arrival. I'm scared to step on a scale and my midsection is already losing definition—I'm down to a four pack—but things will be back to normal soon. She's going home tonight, to her real home.

"Run-of-the-mill wedding date. The chick is young, probably wants to impress her ex or something. She's going to be more nervous than Theo. I ran a check, she's a good girl." Rico winks because we both know good girls are the freakiest. "He'll be home by midnight."

I consider texting Leeyan to let her know Theo's schedule. I've done enough. It's time to distance myself from Leeyan. She'll figure things out on her own. All I can do is make sure I'm there for Theo. He's my priority now.

"What's up with Brazil? You making progress?"

"Yep." I shove a pile of arugula into my mouth.

Rico waits for me to finish chewing, like I have more to say.

"What?"

"Has the glamour of moving worn off already?"

"I have a lot going on."

"You've been working like a beast—is your dick sore yet?"

"Not all dates end with sex."

"Then you're not doing it right, son!" Rico laughs at his comment. "For real, though, are you still all in on Rio?"

If anything could make Rico Team Brazil, it would be me playing house with Leeyan.

"I'm learning Portuguese."

"Is it hard?"

"Not really." I've only completed fifteen percent of the program, but I'll let Rico believe I'm practically fluent. What does he know anyway?

"I should learn a second language. Women love bilingual men. Shit, if you can do it..." he says, taking a cheap shot at my learning ability. "I can start marketing you as a Brazilian lover, make a little more green before you fly the coop."

Rico is always looking out for number one. As much as I want to believe he'll miss me, I know he's going to miss the money I make for him more.

CHAPTER THIRTEEN

Trance is packed tonight. I make three hundred dollars on the stage and another two hundred when I give special attention to a bride-to-be at a VIP table. I don't book a single private. That's my punishment for missing shifts the last two weeks. I'm lucky Jim even let me have a solo.

My shift ended an hour ago. I'm just hanging out, trying to get laid. After two weeks of living with Leeyan, the most untouchable woman on the planet, I'm ready for more. The fact that I've been able to keep my dick in check is a personal accomplishment. It proves I can have a non-sexual relationship with a woman who isn't paying for my time. Theo and Sylvie had a friends-with-benefits thing going and now they're friends. Miracles do happen.

I return to the VIP table with a round of shots. The bride slides her had across my thigh and inches toward my dick. I spread my legs a little wider and place my arm around her, like I'm cuddling her on a couch. Her veil is crooked and one of her eyelashes has come unglued.

"You're hot." She breathes tequila breath into my ear as she palms the head of my dick. I try not to react. I don't want her bridal party to catch on. Even though she considers these women her most trusted friends, her tribe, I'll bet a thousand dollars one of them wants to fuck her man and watching her jerk off a stripper is just the ammo needed to blow up her life and swoop in on the fiancé.

"Whose phone is this?" A woman across the table bends over and picks up a cell phone from the floor.

My hand goes to my pocket.

Fuck.

"Mine."

Cell phones in the main room are a huge no-no, but Theo is on his first side job and I want to make sure he can reach me in case something goes wrong. That's a lie. Leeyan is going to show up on his doorstep tonight, so I want to make sure I'm there for him, and for her.

When I see Theo's number on the screen, I jump up.

"Dain!" I stop him as he walks by. "Ladies, my partner in crime will keep you company while I tend to some business."

Dain slides into the booth and the ladies forget I exist. They don't want me any more than I want them. I'm just a body, an object. To me, they're nothing more than an ATM.

I answer as I walk toward the bar.

Theo rambles about running into one of his regulars at a hotel. "She handed me fifteen hundred dollars and I walked out. I feel like I owe her more than a conversation. What should I do? Should I give the money back?"

"Are you fucking kidding me? Keep the money," I yell. I have one finger in my ear to drown out the music. "Get out of there before you grow a conscience. Think of Lulu."

I give him the spiel about people getting paid for their time. Lawyers and doctors get top dollar for consultations. It's the same for us. Sometimes a woman just needs a man to listen.

"Unless you really want to fuck her..."

"Of course not," Theo says.

"Did she hit on you?"

"Not really, but I'm pretty sure she would fuck me." Theo's right—she would fuck him. He's fuckable.

I'm not fuckable. I'm the best friend, the good listener. If things work out between Theo and Leeyan, I'll be a hero, the one who brought them back together.

"Go home, Theo. You have a beautiful girl waiting for you."

I head back to the VIP table. The bride-to-be and Dain are gone.

"She paid for a private." The woman who found my phone pushes a shot glass in front of me.

She's a short dirty blonde with brown eyes, a plain Jane, the duff of the group.

"Thanks." I lift the glass and take the shot with her. "What's your name?"

"Marnie. I'm the maid of honor." She hiccups. "I set this up—the party bus, the cocaine, everything—and this is what I get." She gestures to the passed-out girl on her left. "Shouldn't I be the one getting laid tonight?"

I can make that happen.

"Things aren't too bad—you have me." I pretend to be kidding, like my ego isn't holding a gun to his head ready to pull the trigger because Marnie doesn't think I'm hot.

She reaches across the table to touch my hand. "I didn't mean your company wasn't good enough."

I offer a smug smile, sighing in relief on the inside.

"I'm a little heated. They're all off in private rooms and I'm playing babysitter to the future sister-in-law."

I move around the table to sit beside Marnie. We could both use a little company right now.

"I was ditched tonight too."

"Who would be dumb enough to ditch you?"

I shake it off. "Doesn't matter now. She's gone."

"She's an idiot."

"She's actually pretty smart." And beautiful. And funny.

What the fuck, Gio?

Why are you sitting here moping about Leeyan fucking Flores?

"You're telling me there's a woman somewhere out there who chose not to be with you?"

"Yes." I won't elaborate; I just want to sulk for a few more hours.

"Do you have a secret flaw that would make her want to leave?" Marnie pretends to look me over. "Let me smell your breath."

"What? No." I lean back.

"Come on, there must be something wrong with you—unless she gave you the good old *it isn't you, it's me* line."

I'm misleading Marnie, but I don't care. Self-loathing always feels good with a partner. It would feel even better if we were naked.

"Do you want to get out of here?"

Marnie pulls back slightly. "You mean like to a private room?"

"No, I mean out of the club. We can go for a walk."

Or back to my place.

Marnie isn't a supermodel or even an Old Navy model, but she'll do.

"Uh, I don't think that's a good idea. I can't leave her." She scoots closer to the comatose chick and starts looking around—you know, like, for help. I completely misread this entire conversation.

"Oh, yeah. You should stay with her." I stand and wave to the dud by the bar. "The next round is on me."

"You don't have to do that." Marnie looks at me like I'm a sad sack.

"Don't worry about it. Enjoy the rest of the night."

I beeline to the locker room to change. I'm so off my game, the safest place for me right now is home.

***

My computer is ringing as I walk through the door. Only one person calls at this hour—Antonia. I could have answered it, but I'm not in the mood. I won't be able to muster the enthusiasm she requires. Pretending I'm jacked about moving to Brazil just ain't happening right now. I don't want to admit this, but Rico was right: I'm not feeling Brazil. It could be Leeyan or my parents losing their home, but I need time to refocus before I talk to Antonia.

I set the pizza box on the kitchen counter and the bathroom to shower. All of Leeyan's things are gone. Seeing the empty slot where her toothbrush should be stings in a way I never thought possible.

It's just a fucking toothbrush!

I've never had a roommate and I'm an only child, so flying solo comes naturally. Now that I've had a taste of companionship, the thought of being alone makes my eyes burn.

Fuck it. I'm just going to admit it.

I like Leeyan.

She's messy in every way a woman can be: in the bathroom, in life, in love—especially love—but she's also fun to be around. I wonder where our lives would be if we had been friends from the jump, if I was a better friend to Theo. If I had supported his relationship with Leeyan instead of resenting it, things might have worked out between them. Theo might have stayed in school. I would have stayed there with him and never worked at Trance. My father wouldn't loathe me.

An overwhelming feeling of loneliness hits me in the gut. The only thing saving me from falling apart is the pepperoni pizza in the other room. I toss on a pair of shorts before heading to the kitchen because I don't eat naked. That's weird.

I flip the box open and rip off a slice.

Come to daddy.

Grease runs down my hand as I fold the gooey slice in half. The few seconds before the pizza hits my tongue is torture. I can taste the spicy sweet sauce on my lips, but before I can shove the entire thing into my mouth, someone knocks on the door.

Fred is supposed to announce all visitors. Whoever is at my door must live in the building, and since I'm a shitty fucking neighbor, I ignore the knocking.

I stuff the slice in my mouth, and it tastes better than sex feels.

I pick up another slice.

Another knock.

Fuck off, I'm eating pizza!

Another knock.

This one is in code. Three short knocks, slight pause, two knocks, and then one more. That was Theo's secret code. He came up with it in college. My time there was brief, but my sexual conquests were many.

I drop the pizza and open the door.

It's Leeyan.

And she's crying.

"Are you all right?" I take her arm. "What happened?"

"I just made a fool of myself." She walks to the kitchen, opens the cabinet, and pulls out the whiskey. She doesn't even bother with a glass, just shoots it right out of the bottle. "He's in love with Sylvie."

"What are you talking about?"

"Theo, he's in love with Sylvie. They're together," she spits out—literally. Whiskey sprays my chin. She opens the cabinet again and removes a glass. "I went there to beg for forgiveness. I was ready to swallow my pride for a chance to be a family," she cries. "But the truth is, I don't want him. I just want Lulu."

"You don't have to be with Theo to have a relationship with Lulu."

She takes a drink like her glass is filled with ice-cold water, not room-temperature whiskey.

"I thought if he took me back, if he forgave me, maybe Lulu would too."

"Did you see her?"

"Yes." She's crying even harder. "She's so amazing. Why didn't you tell me how incredible she was?"

"You have to witness Lulu firsthand to really get it."

"I want to hate Theo, but he knocked it out of the park with that little girl." She shakes her head in dismay. "Does he do *anything* wrong? Tell me he's a porn addict or something. He can't be the perfect father."

"Other than being broke and barely making rent, Theo is the best dad I know."

Leeyan sighs then wipes her cheek on the sleeve of her hoodie.

"You're right. I have to win her back on my own."

Last I checked, this wasn't a competition.

"Honestly, I'm relieved." Leeyan grabs a clean glass and fills it halfway. She places it in front of me.

I take a sip.

"Knowing he's in love with someone else kind of lets me off the hook. Now I can just focus on getting my daughter back. It won't be easy, but now that I've seen Lulu, I fully understand what I've missed. I was a fool to believe she didn't want me in her life."

Her eyes fill with pride. I think for the first time in Leeyan's life, the idea of being a mom feels right.

"How did Lulu react when she saw you?"

"She was timid. Sylvie encouraged her to sit with me." She pulls her phone and shows me a selfie. "We look alike."

They do. So much more than I ever realized.

"Lulu looks happy." I'm not lying. I know the kid, that smile is one hundred.

"I only agreed to stay because Lulu didn't want me to leave. I know what that kind of fears is like. Being afraid your mother will leave and not come back. I won't repeat that cycle. I'll fight. I'll do anything it takes to be with my daughter."

Fathers come and go out of their children's lives. If they are given leniency because they weren't ready to be parents. Then women should be awarded the same. Just because Leeyan carried Lulu for nine months, that doesn't mean she was psychologically prepared to be a parent. She's the first to admit she screwed up. Everyone deserves a second chance. Even the assholes.

I see that woman inside of her, the one fighting to come out.

"When do I get to meet her?"

She looks up. Her eyes are all lit, her face is glowing. "You helped create her."

My phone buzzes; I ignore it. Nothing is going to tempt me away from this apartment.

"I didn't do anything—except let you sleep on my really uncomfortable couch."

"Your couch sucks." She tweaks her back in a playful response. "Really, Gio. You have me time to get my shit together. I really appreciate you."

"I was just here to kick some balls." I try not to blush, but I feel my face warm. "You don't give yourself enough credit."

"Speaking of credit." An evil grin spreads across Leeyan's face. "I still need to collect on my dance."

I suck in a breath—me, the dude. My breath hitches at the look of playful desire on Leeyan's pretty face. If there was ever a moment to let feelings take control, this is it.

She moved out.

I'm moving to Brazil.

On a scale of bad ideas, this pegs the meter.

I play it cool, like Mr. Grey. "All right let me clean up first."

"Yeah, cause sloppy seconds ain't my style," she sasses.

"Try sloppy fourths." I step around her.

She pushes my hand off her shoulder. "Ew."

CHAPTER FOURTEEN

I prison shower—only the important areas, and in record time. When I return to the living room, Leeyan has it staged for my performance.

My desk chair sits in the center of the room.

The lights are dimmed.

Music plays on the surround sound.

A bottle of Jameson sits on the counter beside two glasses, each filled a quarter of the way, a single ice cube in one.

She springs up from the couch.

"Wait there."

She turns off the light above the stove in the kitchen then picks up the glasses.

"Cheers." I toss back the entire glass.

She's going to get her money's worth with interest. Tonight isn't just about pleasing a client; I have my own fantasy to fulfill. Now that I know Theo has completely moved on, I get my chance. The one I blew the night I was late to the club.

Leeyan sets her glass on the counter.

"Where do you want me?"

I take her hand and lead her to the chair. I make sure the wheels are locked then guide her into the seat. She's giddy and silly, like someone just pulled her on stage at a magic show. She's treating this like it's a joke, but she changed her clothes. She's in easy-access sweats and a pink sports tank with a built-in bra.

An Ed Sheeran song comes on, it isn't something I usually dance to. When I try to change it, she stops me.

"No, I like this."

"I'm not feeling his vibe." I pick up my phone and scroll through the list.

"I paid for this, so I should have a say in the music."

"It doesn't work that way, honey." I'm in full suave mode. "Don't worry, you'll be happy with what I choose."

"Can you choose something by Ed Sheeran?" Her persistence is cute. It also turns me on. She has a fantasy too, and I'm all about making dreams come true.

"Okay." I scroll back to a song I had considered for a routine. It's bluesy and rarely played on the radio, which is why I didn't use it. I want my songs played everywhere. I want women to hear them and remember me. Return customers pay the bills.

The song begins and I spin around in full character. Her silly grin slips into a look of desire. We don't break eye contact as I cross the room. I stand in front of her, slowly swaying my hips, my hand runs over her head, and then she does something I'm not ready for.

She stands up.

Her arms snake around my neck. We hold each other politely and move to the music. She pulls back to look at me. Her hand lingers on my neck. The other hand raises my shirt. I take the hint. I pull it off and toss it on the floor then run my hand through her hair, something I've wanted to do for weeks. We touch and look at each other in every way we've avoided since she got here.

When I can't take another second of being this close, I lift her into my arms and spin her around before setting her down in front of the couch. She goes up on her tiptoes to press her lips to my ear. My eyes close and I rub my head against hers like a cat begging for attention. She slides back down to her normal height, her lips tracing my neck. I bury my face in her hair. She smells like me, and a woman who smells like Old Spice Swagger wouldn't normally turn me on, but she's the exception.

We stay in this moment, live in it as the song continues to play.

My hands on her face.

Her lips on my chest.

I don't even try to hide my arousal. Even if I wanted to, I couldn't. She's pressed against me. I feel her chest rise with every breath she takes.

"Gio," she finally says.

I angle my head to see her face, the face I've looked forward to seeing every day for the past two weeks. She places her hand on my cheek, and I mirror her movement. She's in control—she always has been. I pull her closer and bend at the knees so she has a better look into my soul.

She doesn't speak, her eyes watching my mouth. As soon as she makes her move, my eyes close. When her lips find mine, something in my chest unlocks and flutters out. Our lips get acquainted before she introduces her tongue. Her mouth is small, soft, succulent. I could kiss her for hours.

"I want more," she whispers.

I carry her to the room and lay her on my bed. She lifts her hips and pulls her sweats off. She's wearing plain white panties. When you have a woman in your bed who can rock white cotton panties, you've hit the jackpot.

I crawl up the bed and end up with my face in her vagina. She moans, which tells me I'm doing things right. Leeyan has been with women, who were better at this than me. I twirl my tongue and she arches her back. Her hands find my head. I move my mouth faster, my tongue deeper. Just when I think she's going to come, she pulls me up for air.

"Fuck me," she demands.

Most of the women I fuck relinquish their control to me. They want to be ravished. I'm the lion, they're the lamb. Leeyan is not that kind of woman. She is vocal. She's the alpha.

I pull my shorts off and kneel in between her legs. I take a few seconds to look at her, watch her. Small lines—stretch marks—stripe her abdomen. Her breasts are small and round, nipples dark and hard. I've imagined her naked body while I showered, while she slept, but nothing could have prepared me for the naturally beautiful woman lying beneath me.

"Gio." Her voice draws me back.

I lower myself to kiss her, the head of my dick brushes against her, and my mouth melts into hers.

"You feel so good," I moan.

My words are natural, real. Nothing happening right now was negotiated or paid for. Nothing about this moment is fake.

She pushes on my chest and I open my eyes. "Don't you think we should use a condom?"

Oh shit.

The last thing I need is a surprise baby. I open the drawer on the nightstand and pull out a foil-wrapped lifesaver. I rip it open and slide it on with one hand.

"Did you practice that move?" Leeyan teases.

"No—yes." I've had lots of practice, but I don't want to think about those encounters. They were business; this is pleasure.

"Are you ready?" I ask, as if we're about to jump out of an airplane. That's what this feels like: fear and adrenaline.

"Are you?" she counters, legs spread open, waiting for me to slide inside.

I'm hard and ready for what comes next. I hope it isn't me.

I want this to last.

I want to be her last.

This train of thought reminds me of her first. The realization that I'm about to go inside of Theo's ex-girlfriend hits me.

I'm going to have sex with Leeyan.

I'm inches away, several inches, from breaking the number one bro code. Leeyan squirms impatiently beneath me.

She wants me.

Me.

The guy she met on the roof of Oasis.

I center my hips with hers and push forward. I slip easily inside. The condom is lubed, but mostly it's her. She's wet for me.

We kiss as we make love. It's new to me. I try not to kiss while I fuck. When I do, the kisses are short and hard, but Leeyan seems to enjoy my tongue just as much as my cock. I feel closer, deeper in her than any woman I've ever been with. She's blowing my mind.

I kiss Leeyan deeper, pump harder. I hook my right hand under her knee and use it for leverage. She reaches for my head, pulling me back to her mouth. She sucks my tongue and my body goes into spasms as I have the best orgasm of my life.

She continues to kiss me, knowing I've already come.

That's when I realize she didn't.

Fuck me.

I roll off her and remove the used condom. I toss it on the floor and reach into the drawer for a new one.

"Seriously?" She props herself up on her elbows to inspect my dick. "He doesn't look ready for round two."

"Give me a minute." I stand and head to the bathroom.

"Gio, wait." She sits up. "You don't have to do it for me."

"Do what?" I play dumb.

She sighs and bites her lip. I feel a confession coming on.

"I saw the bottle in the cabinet."

She doesn't have to elaborate.

"I wasn't going to..." I stop before the lie slips out. Why bother? She knows. "But you didn't..."

"It's not worth taking the pill. I don't want an altered version of you." She glances at my limp dick. "Don't force it."

I walk back to the bed and sit face to face with Leeyan. "The little blue pill doesn't force anything. It's still all me."

Her hand is on my wet, limp noodle so fast I don't have time to protect myself. "This is you." She repositions her grip. "When you're ready, we'll go again and again." She kisses my chin then gently bites me. I begin to stiffen in her hand, and she feels it. "See."

I grab her arms and force her onto her back, her hands above her head. I lick her neck then move lower to her nipples. I circle them with my tongue, and she bucks in response. I place my knee between her legs so she has something to push back against. I keep licking until her moaning peaks and she comes.

Now I'm ready for round two. I curse the condom as I put it on and understand, finally, why men hate these slippery little things. I want to feel Leeyan inside and out. Even through the condom, the torturous sensation is almost too much to take; I wouldn't last five minutes if I were bare. Imagine the feeling you get when your foot falls asleep and you try to walk; it tickles to the point of pain. Sex the second time around, just minutes after coming, feels euphoric, better than any drug or pill could offer.

It's nearly dawn when I finally lie down to sleep with Leeyan cuddled in my arms beneath my six-hundred-dollar sheets.

"These are ruined," I tease as I tuck the sheet around her.

"It's just a sheet."

I don't want to drop the price tag and sound like a douche. I'm a douche for even thinking about it.

"If there's one thing I've learned over the last three years, it's that things don't matter. I had nothing when I left for the army. Everything I needed, the army provided—food, clothes, a bed."

I've built my life around things, replacing people with clothes, cars, and money. Those *things* have never let me down.

"When it boils down to it, people don't need much, they *want*. I wouldn't lay my life down for this country to protect a man's car or a house. We don't fight to protect things—we fight for people. Tomorrow, I'm going to start fighting."

I feel like a line is about to be drawn, one I won't be able to straddle. If I have to pick a side, someone is going to get hurt. Odds are, that someone is me.

"I want to kick myself for not seeing her sooner. If I had..."

"Don't look back. You're not going in that direction."

Leeyan kisses my hand. "Did you read that somewhere?"

"I did." I kiss her shoulder. "It was on a sign at the gym."

"Looking forward isn't always the best thing either. I had tunnel vision when it came to the army. No matter where I went in the world, knowing she was here tainted it all. There is nothing more powerful than family. Running away doesn't cut the ties. You'll always be tethered to the people you love."

I think of my parents. Moving to Brazil won't change the way my father feels about me. He'll always be here, waiting for my return, waiting to tell me the new ways I've disappointed him. Unlike Leeyan, the strings tying me here are weak.

"I hope you aren't trying to tell me something." I squeeze her.

"I'm just saying, your parents will still be your parents no matter where you live." She's using my own words on me.

"I may be an ambitious idiot, but I feel like Brazil is my chance to be more, have more, have it all—success, respect, money."

"Love?"

A small bead of sweat runs down my forehead. "Love isn't a priority."

"Really? So, you want respect without caring?"

"I'd rather be feared than loved." I laugh and wait to see if she gets the movie reference. "It's a line from *A Bronx Tale*."

"I know. It's stupid."

"If you didn't just give me the best orgasm of my life, I'd kick you out of this bed."

She twists to face me. "The best?"

"Oh jeez, don't get cocky."

"You said it." She looks cocky—cocky and beautiful. "For the record, you are on my top two list."

I look at her like *What the fuck?*

"Like out of two, I'm number one."

She rolls her eyes in the sassiest way a woman can roll her eyes. I want to see them roll again, this time while

177

I'm inside her. I flip her onto her back and hold her arms at her sides, my body pressed to hers so she can't move.

"What do I have to do to earn the number one spot?" We lock eyes. "Tell me what you want, Leeyan."

Her face is sad, the opposite of what she should look like right now.

"I want a happy ending, but I don't think I deserve one."

"What does your happily ever after look like?"

"Every morning I wake up to find my husband cooking breakfast for the kids. I'm a cop, and he's a stay-at-home dad."

Apparently, I'm not in this fantasy.

"We live in the same house forever, the kind where we mark the wall with the height of our children and never paint over it. I lived in so many places until I met Louisa, and I don't want Lulu to have that kind of childhood."

"She doesn't." It isn't my place to have this conversation with her. Hell, I'm not even the man of her dreams.

"Tell me about Brazil?" She changes the subject.

I don't really want to discuss anything to do with Antonia while I'm lying naked in bed with Leeyan.

"Are you excited? Do you have a place? Tell me about the job."

"I have an apartment in Ipanema, across the street from the beach. The view is everything you expect, ocean as far as you can see." I'm no longer thinking of the beach as I watch her face light with excitement.

"Maybe I'll visit you—if you want me to." She tries to play coy.

"With Lulu?"

"Sure. Kids love the beach."

I won't tell her Lulu hates the beach; she'll have to find out on her own. "What will you tell Lulu?"

"What do you mean? Can't I visit a friend?"

"We aren't friends, not to them." Meaning to anyone outside of my apartment. The world believes we're enemies, but here we are, legs entwined, my cock resting on her thigh.

"This feels like the beginning of something, and it scares the shit out of me." She looks at me for help. "Am I right?"

Leeyan watches my eyes, waiting for me to decide if we have a chance, a future. Even though this feels like the beginning of a happily ever after, I have to lie and tell her it's only a happy for now.

CHAPTER FIFTEEN

I'm driving to the gym when Mom calls to ask if I want a box of old toys. She's preparing for their eviction even though Josie said the buyer pulled out.

"This is a buyer's market, Giovanni. Someone will be along again soo—" She cuts out. "Hold on, it's my call waiting." She clicks over before I have a chance to object.

She returns a beat later. "Gio?"

"Yeah, Ma. I'm driving."

"Oh, then just come over. I'm making eggplant parm."

"I can't, I have errands to run."

"You can bring your friend, Lee." She's referring to Leeyan, even though I know she knows who she is.

"I'm not with her—I mean, she's moved...on."

Leeyan moved into Theo's building. The favor she didn't want to cash in on was with Dennis. Since Theo is in her old apartment, Dennis agreed to let Leeyan move in upstairs.

We didn't make plans to see each other or even talk the morning she left. I didn't want her to feel as if she owed me anything. I told her to focus on Lulu. Really, I did it for myself. What went down in my bedroom that night was next level. I'm comfortable on my level—leaving it open, no strings. The last thing I need is more strings. My visa was approved. Everything is falling into place.

"Well that's okay. She was complicated, as you kids say."

Exactly.

"Come before six, before your father gets home, okay? Bye."

I'm back on meal prep, so the last thing I need is Mom's cheesy eggplant parmesan. It does sound good, though, and I could use some comfort food. Lying to my best friend is stressing me out. Theo is with Sylvie now, but who knows, maybe a few months down the line he wants Leeyan back. Maybe she wants him. I don't want one night of mind-blowing sex to ruin their chance to be a family. Our lives are headed in opposite directions with no way of intersecting. There's no need for Leeyan and I to pretend it was more than sex.

I cut my workout short because the only thing on my mind is food. When I get to the locker room, my phone is buzzing in my bag.

It's Theo.

"Dude! Where the fuck have you been?" He's anxious. "Shit is going down in a major way, bro."

I've been waiting for this call, dreading it. I could be a man, admit she was hiding at my place for weeks, but it will do more harm than good.

When he comes up for air, I give him a: "Damn, dude. That's crazy."

He rambles some more about him and Sylvie being a thing and how he put his dick on Leeyan's leg by accident.

"Leeyan was acting, I don't know, jealous...like she wanted me back. I can't go down that rabbit hole again."

"You really think she wants you back?" I do a piss-poor job of not sounding jealous, but Theo probably mistakes it for concern.

"Don't worry, I'm all in with Sylvie. She's the love of my life."

I've heard all this before with Leeyan. Theo is the one who needs a new set of balls. The boy falls hard.

"Now she's living above me and I don't know if I can trust her with Lulu."

I jump at the chance to defend Leeyan. "Give her a chance. If nothing else, you get help with the rug rat, and I don't know, maybe Lulu needs Leeyan."

Theo is quiet. I worry I laid it on too thick.

"You're right," he finally says. "I mean, shit, she's Lulu's mom—even though she fucking bailed on her."

I bite my tongue. Standing up for Leeyan is the last thing I would do—the old Gio, not the Gio who has licked every inch of her body.

"I gotta go, bro. I'm going to my parents' place."

"Tell them I said hi and sorry I haven't brought Lulu around in a while."

We hang up and my first instinct is to call Leeyan, but I don't want to come off as playing both sides. This was inevitable. Theo is my best friend, and Leeyan is...well, complicated.

Mom is sweeping the porch when I pull up. Since Dad is still at work, I block the driveway. Mom stops and leans on her broom as she watches me parallel park. A woman walks out of the empty house next door, and Mom steps inside and closes the door.

I'm barely out of my car when the woman starts speaking to me.

"I hope you're not here for the open house—we just closed up." Her hand is extended. "I'm Maureen Shafer, City Lights Realty."

I take her card.

"Also, I think we might have an offer on the table." She crosses her fingers. "But this one"—she gestures to my house—"this one is a gem. Untouched, original woodwork, oak floors—a virgin."

I play with her a little. "Is it rented?"

"Yes, but if you plan to live here"—she winks—"owner move-in will solve that problem."

That problem. My parents are *that problem.*

"What are they asking?"

"It's a fair price." She looks back at the house, ready to pull a number out of her ass. "Eight," she tosses out. When I don't bite, she blurts out, "Seven fifty is their absolute lowest. At that price, it won't be on the market for long."

"Will I be able to see it?"

She moves closer to whisper, "The seller is really attached to the old couple who rents the property. They've lived here forever." She rolls her eyes. "She wants to respect their privacy, yadda."

"But you're taking offers?"

"Yes, and I have pictures online." She flips open her messenger bag and pulls out a flyer. "Showings are done by appointment only."

Maureen continues down the street to collect her sandwich sign, and I look at the flyer. The photos of my parents' outdated furniture sit in little squares with captions that read: "charming", "designer's dream", "vintage accents". I don't see a large kitchen with great potential. I see the stove my mother has spent most of my life standing at, making every meal of my childhood, the arch to the living room I helped Mom decorate every year for Christmas, the dining room table my parents received as a wedding gift from my grandparents. I crumple the flyer and shove it in my pocket as I walk inside. I find mom in the kitchen. She already has two containers packed for me, sitting on the counter.

"Hey, Ma." I walk up behind her and kiss her cheek. Her face is red, like she's been crying. Rather than ask why or tell her about the real estate agent outside, I talk about food. Food is safe.

"I don't need that much food."

"Who's going to eat it here? We're only two people."

"Why do you make so much?"

"I don't know how to make less. The recipe is for a family, not two people." She's laying the guilt on thicker than the cheese in the dish she's covering with foil.

"Okay, Ma." I pat her shoulder and sit at the table. I pull out my phone to see if Leeyan has sent me a text. She'd love my mom's eggplant parmesan. It'll make a tasty post-sex meal. It was my idea to leave things open, but it stings every time I check my phone and don't see her name.

"The box is on the floor in your room." Mom reminds me why I'm here. "I was going to toss it, but some things you could sell on the internet. I don't know, make some money."

"It's just a bunch of old junk."

"Maybe." She shrugs. "That's for you to decide."

My childhood bed was replaced with a futon right after I moved out. Mom uses this room for crafting, knitting, or whatever old ladies do. The box is on the floor next to a desk—one that looks familiar.

"Hey Ma, when'd you get this desk?" I examine the drawers.

She appears in the doorway. "It's from IKEA." She pronounces it *hi-key-ya*.

"I know—*when* did you get it? You guys should be getting rid of old furniture, not buying more."

I've never really seen my mother angry. Sure, I got in trouble as a kid, but just kid stuff, nothing that caused her to look at me the way she is now.

"Your father bought it on clearance. It didn't come with the instructions, so he went on the internet."

It's just like my old man to buy an IKEA desk on clearance. It's already cheap as hell. I start rummaging through the box of old toys and find an old Transformer that could be worth something along with a stack of baseball cards.

"Remember this?" I hold up a baseball I signed when I was ten and we put it in a plastic trophy case. "I really thought it would be worth something one day."

"It's nice." Mom wipes her hands on the apron around her waist. It's her nervous tick. "He found a video."

"One of my high school games?"

"Giovanni," Mom snaps. "He found *the* video."

"Yeah, I heard you."

I start making a pile of things I want to keep on the desk.

"The video was you, Gio." Her tone changes from anger to pain. "Building a desk in your underwear." My mother, for the first time in my life, stares at me in disappointment, shame.

"What do you mean?" Playing dumb doesn't help.

"It was you and another boy in your underwear." She sighs and wipes her already dry hands again. "Your father saw everything. He only allowed me to see your face on the screen because I didn't believe him. He watched it all...everything."

I go from embarrassment to defense mode.

"There was nothing to see. I put together a desk, so what?" I repack the box and walk out of the room. "I made a lot of money that day—did he see that?"

Mom follows me to the kitchen. "It isn't about money, Gio. Your dignity—"

"My dignity?" I spit as I pick up the containers. "He's the one who cleans other people's shit and piss all day long. So what if I put together a desk in my underwear? At least those men respect me."

That's a lie. Those motherfuckers recorded us. They broke the rules and will be banned from The Agency.

"You're an object to them," Mom argues.

"I'd rather be an object than nothing."

Mom glances at the clock, a subtle cue that I should go before the old man gets here. Even though leaving is for my own good, it hurts that she wants me to go. Me being here makes her life harder and my choices easier.

"I gotta go, Ma." I kiss her cheek and she pats my arms. "I love you."

She takes my face in her hands and kisses my cheeks. "I love you, *patanino*."

There was a time I went months without seeing them. I lived on the other side of the city, but it could've been the other side of the world. Moving to Brazil won't change my relationship with my parents. Nothing can salvage this sinking ship.

Mom usually walks me outside and waves as I drive off, but not today. She kisses me goodbye at the door and goes back inside. I have a feeling she's hiding, and as I get in my car, I see why. Josie waves from across the street. She must be visiting Maggie. I place the food containers in the trunk then go say hi.

"How are you, Miss Josie?" I hug her.

"I'll never get over how tall you got." She gives me a squeeze. Josie's curly red hair is peppered with gray, her waist a little thicker. "Picking up food from your mom?"

"You know how she is." I look back at the house and wonder if she's peeking at us through the curtains.

"I do." Josie smiles in reverie. "I'm going to miss her cooking."

"Then why are you kicking them out?" I don't mean to sound cold. "Can't you work something out so they can stay?"

"I offered them the house, they didn't want it." She shrugs like there is nothing more she can do.

"They can't afford it." I feel emotions creeping to the surface—guilt, anger, pride. "You can raise the rent if you need to—I'll pay the difference." I shouldn't be making these kinds of promises. My father would kill me if he knew I made this offer. He'd move just to spite me.

"It isn't about the money, Giovanni. We're old and tired. This city is for the young. We just want out, a nice quiet place in the country."

Easy for her to say; she's rich. My parents have nothing, but that isn't Josie's fault. She's done so much for my family already. The rent on our house has been the same for nearly a decade.

"This is a great house to raise a family in." She gives me that mom-like look. "Are you dating?"

Josie has been trying to set me up with one of her daughters since before I had hair on my balls.

"I'm seeing someone," I lie, but the truth is, I want to see her. I miss her.

"That's good." She pats my shoulder. "If you have a friend looking for a house, let me know. I'd love to keep it in the family, but my girls want to live in the sun—except Maggie. She's nostalgic."

"Tell Mags I said hi."

She goes inside, leaving me alone on the street.

I wonder if Theo would be interested in buying the place and renting it to my parents, but that's ridiculous—he can't afford it. Nobody I consider a friend has the cash to buy a house and let my parents live in it for less than half the monthly mortgage payment. I'm already too invested in Antonia, and the last thing I need is her having power over my parents.

This is on me and my first instinct is to run.

CHAPTER SIXTEEN

I text Antonia and ask if she has time to talk. We set up a video call twenty minutes later.

"*Olá*," I say to show off.

"*Como vai?*" She asks if everything is good. "You're worried—I can see it in your forehead."

I look at my face in the little square on the bottom of the screen. My forehead looks normal.

"You never call me unless it's something." She lights a cigarette and takes a long drag. "Speak!"

"I have a favor to ask," I start.

Her left eyebrow goes up as she rests her elbow on the desk in anticipation.

"Do you think I can keep my apartment after I move to Rio?"

"Why?" She's always direct and to the point. There's no bullshitting Antonia. "You think you will fail?"

"No! Nothing like that." I make a *psh* sound. I've debated whether to tell her I want to move my parents in after I leave. If she knows they're here, it gives her so much more leverage over me. "I want to have a place when I come back to visit."

She nods slowly, like she's not really buying it. "Your parents have a home, no? Can't you stay with them or in a hotel? If it's just a visit."

"You know better than anyone that having a place of your own is so much nicer, and I'll continue to pay rent."

She waves her hand in front of the screen. "It isn't the money, you know this. I don't care about the money. If I did, you wouldn't be paying half of what the apartment is worth." The little slip tells me I was right.

"I could have Fred hook me up with the owner's information and him or her directly if you think that's okay."

She smiles like she's been caught in a lie. "Okay then. You can keep the place."

"Thank you, Antonia." I try to exude as much gratitude as one can through video chat. "I know you're busy."

"No, no." She waves her finger in the camera. The evil grin on her face tells me she isn't done with me. I just hope her dirty mind is thinking doesn't involve nudity.

"I have a favor, too."

"Uh, okay." I brace for whatever humiliation she's about to lay on me.

"Lenny Niemeyer is meeting with designers at a cocktail party in San Francisco. I want you to go there and convince her to meet with me."

Lenny Niemeyer is one of Brazil's top swimsuit designers, and Antonia has been trying to work with her for years.

"I...I don't even know how to get invited to something like that," I mumble. "When is the party?"

"Now. I'll text you the name of the bar. It's a casual meet and greet. Men like you don't need an invitation—not with that face."

"What do I say?"

"Tell her she's a fool not to work with me. Brazil is a mecca for beach fashion. California is..." She grunts in disgust. "College kids cannot design couture."

I like her last comment. I bank it to use for later and agree to try. I'll go to the bar, speak to this woman, and do my best to convince her Antonia is the next big thing—a favor for a favor.

The best part of this fiasco is choosing my outfit. Bumming around in jeans and t-shirts is nice, but I get off on dressing up. I decide on a Prada two-tone blue polo shirt with the Gucci jacket I lifted from the fashion show. It fits like a glove, even with the extra pounds. My jeans, not so much. I opt for a loose-fitting pair of Diesels—there's no way I'm squeezing my ass into skinny jeans. Lastly, I slip on a pair of Versace Colorblock sneakers, because you can pull off a "casual" shoe when they cost just under a grand.

I get the text from Antonia. The bar is in the fashion district, probably an old warehouse turned brewery. I order an Uber and head downstairs.

"Looking sharp, youngblood!" Fred is standing by the desk with a fly swatter. "Looks like you're catching a big fish tonight."

I pound his fist. "You know it."

I miss this feeling—cocky and sure.

Leeyan has me all soft and gooey. Okay, not *all* soft.

After one-and-done for so long, I forgot what new sex was like, how good it feels to explore someone's body for the sake of doing it. You'd think after three or four times it gets repetitive; it doesn't. Every time was better than the last. Thinking about her gets me hard.

I adjust my junk as the Uber pulls to a stop outside my building.

"How ya doin?" The driver is male, dark-haired, and foreign. "Nice shoes."

"Thanks." I don't like to chat, so I take my phone out and pretend to check something important like Facebook.

"There's a little traffic—are you in a hurry?"

I look at the parking lot in front of us. "No, no rush."

We move one block in fifteen minutes. I could walk faster. To pass the time, I decide texting Leeyan is safe. She replies immediately.

Me: What's up?

Leeyan: I was just thinking about you.

Me: Good things?

Leeyan: Bad things.

Me: Bad meaning bad or bad meaning good?

Leeyan: :P

She asks about work. I ask about Lulu. I even bring up the weather as I work up the nerve to ask her if she wants to come over tonight.

Leeyan: Can you do me a favor?

Me: Anything

Leeyan: I bought a dresser on Offerup and I need someone to
help me bring it upstairs when it gets delivered today.

Theo must be out, otherwise she wouldn't be asking me to come over.

Me: Sure. When is it going to be delivered?

Leeyan: In an hour.

Fuck my life.

Leeyan: I don't want to leave it on the street. Someone will totally steal it and I can't just sit outside and wait for Theo to come home.

Me: Where is he?

Leeyan: I don't know. He said he had a job. If you can't make it that's fine.

Me: On my way.

I jump out of the Uber and head to the underground trains. It takes less than twenty minutes to get to Leeyan's place. The closer I get to her street, the more I sweat.

When I can see the building, I text her and tell her to come down.

Me: I'm here.

Leeyan: We're at the park.

We, meaning her and Lulu. Now I know this is a bad idea. The park is directly across the street from Leeyan and Theo's building. If he comes home, I'm busted. I walk up the path to the playground, which is packed with strollers and little people. I spot Lulu standing at the top of a structure. I follow her gaze and find Leeyan.

She's beaming as she watches her daughter play, and her smile doesn't falter when I stop in front of her.

"Hi." She motions to hug me then stops and holds up a melting purple popsicle.

"Hi." I stop myself from touching her. "Is this a good idea?"

I look back to where Lulu is holding court.

"Yeah, we'll say you were stopping by to see Theo and we ran into each other."

Sounds reasonable.

We sit on a bench where Leeyan can keep an eye on Lulu. She's in a long black and white striped skirt, tied in a knot on the side. A black bra is visible through her white t-shirt, and the afternoon breeze tousles her now brown hair. I take a lock between my fingers.

"No more pink?"

She turns to look at me, pulling her hair from my hand.

"Lulu said the moms at her school don't have pink hair."

"She's such a tyrant."

"I probably shouldn't indulge her, but I want her to like me."

What's not to like.

"How are things going with Lulu and Theo?"

"Not bad. I think she's warming up to me a little more every day. I wish I came to see weeks ago."

If she had, we never would have hooked up. I'm an asshole for thinking this, but I'm glad she waited, and I got have Leeyan to myself. As an only child, sharing was never my forte. When I dated in high school and college, the women I chose would give up all their free time to spend with me. Magic dick. Even if being with Leeyan were an option, I don't think it would work out if I had to share her with Lulu. The kid always comes first, even a selfish prick like me knows that.

"How's your Portuguese coming along?" The question has a touch of bitterness, like she's reminding me I'm leaving.

"*Saudades de você.*" I tell her I miss her.

The statement pulls her attention from Lulu. "Damn," she breathes. "Say something else."

"*Não consigo parar de pensar em você,*"

"What does that mean?"

I lie because I don't want to admit the truth, I'm falling for her.

"It means, I'll miss you when I leave."

Her lips form a pout, not a sexy one. Okay, a sexy one. She brings the popsicle to her mouth and slurps off the excess liquid.

"You sucked that like a pro."

She smiles in spite of herself. Leeyan is trying to be the right thing, act the right way, even if it goes against who she really is. Her hair, the outfit, it screams hipster mom.

She licks her finger and looks around for a trash can. "I can't deal with this anymore. I'll just get her a new one."

"I'm kind of enjoying the show. Watching you lick a popsicle...it does things to me." I lean in close until my nose is in her hair.

"Typical male fantasy." She walks to the trash a few feet away with a wiggle in her hips. When she returns to the bench, she sits a little closer.

"You know the key to a good blow job is making the woman think it was her idea."

"Who said anything about a blow job?"

"A dick in your mouth can be a good thing."

"For who?"

She inches away, and my first instinct is to pull her back.

"You and Theo never..."

"We didn't have that kind of relationship."

I nod toward the playground where Lulu is bossing around some older kids. "You were fucking—that much is obvious."

"Sex and blow jobs"—Leeyan holds her hands as if each word is sitting in a palm—"not the same thing."

"Oral sex is sex," I argue. "You've had girlfriends." I consider saying the words I'm visualizing in my head, but having a boner in a park surrounded by kids—not cool.

"That's different. Girls are different."

"That's sexist."

"How does that make me sexist?"

"You'll lick a vagina," I whisper the last word as a gay couple walks by with their Chinese daughter and French bulldog. "But you won't suck a dick—sexist." I mime doing a mic drop.

"This isn't a gender equality issue, it's a preference," Leeyan insists. "I'm not saying I would never suck a dick." Her cheeks flush. "I'm just saying it isn't happening tonight."

There's always tomorrow night.

Leeyan gets a text from the delivery company and we head across the street to her building. Lulu doesn't question why I'm there; she doesn't know any better. She does insist on holding both of our hands so she can swing between us as we walk, which turns into her refusing to put her feet down, so we end up deadlifting her the entire way home.

While Leeyan signs some paperwork, I go upstairs and hang my Gucci jacket in the hall closet. It's worth more than all the furniture in this apartment combined.

The dresser isn't as heavy as she thought, and after we navigate it through the narrow door, we're golden. The apartment is directly above Theo's and is laid out the same way with a long hallway and hardwood floors. We carry the dresser to the only bedroom.

"I think that corner works better," Leeyan directs.

We move it near the window.

I scoot it back until it hits the wall. "It's pretty small for a dresser." It's white with three drawers, kid-sized.

Of course— it's for the kid.

"Perfect." Leeyan gives me a quick kiss on the cheek. "Thanks, Gio."

"My pleasure." I give her a sexy smile, the one that makes her knees weak. I hesitate then start to pull her close. When she doesn't object, I take her in my arms.

"What were you saying about pleasure?" she asks flirtatiously. "Damn, this feels good." She snuggles against me.

"I thought maybe you were over it." *It being me.*

She grabs my ass. "Not even close. What about you?"

I press my hard-on into her stomach. "What do you think?"

Something in the living room falls with a thud. Leeyan pulls away, remembering who she is, and runs out of the room.

It will never just be us again. Even if we steal a day or night alone before I leave, she'll always have Lulu on her mind. Lulu will always be first. That's fine, but I don't want to compete with a kid. It isn't in my nature. I sure as hell won't wait around for crumbs.

My phone buzzes in my pocket.

Oh fuck.

Antonia doesn't know if I made it to the party or not. I can tell her I was late, or they wouldn't let me in. She'll never believe that, though. I hate to use my parents as an excuse, but I'm desperate.

"Hey," I answer, pretending I'm out of breath. "I'm almost there. My mother called…"

She's speaking Portuguese; she's pissed. *"Não pode fazer um favor, idiota!"*

I only pick up the last word. Idiot.

"It's too late! She already left."

How does she know that unless she had someone else at the party? If that's the case, why did she need me?

"I ask a simple favor, Giovanni, one, and you fail. What else will you fail at doing?" She inhales. I imagine her pacing with a cigarette pinched between her perfectly manicured fingers, her hair blowing in all directions. Antonia is wild, in her style and in her personality. "It was *perfeito*, perfect! Nicolette had it all set up. You just had to show her a good time!"

Lulu appears in the doorway. I hold my finger to my mouth so she doesn't speak. She rolls her eyes then closes the door.

"Who is Nicolette?" The question throws her off.

"What? Nicolette is Nicolette. She works for me."

"If Nicolette was there representing you, why did you need me?" I want to hear her say it, hear her admit it.

"Gio, baby, what do you mean?"

"You asked me to go to the party and convince that woman to work with you, but clearly you already had someone there who did that. What would I bring to the table?"

"To the table, nothing." She pauses, takes another drag. "To her bed, something."

"So you're pimping me out now?" I imagine what my life will look like a year from now: me doing *favors* for Antonia in Brazil. "Is the job at the club even real?"

"Yes! Of course. You think I'm lying? You don't want to come to Brazil now?"

I sit on the edge of the bed and look around Leeyan's bedroom. Will I ever be allowed to sleep here? Will I ever be welcome? We're straddling a line that should never be crossed. Once Theo finds out, shit gets real. Losing my best friend isn't something I know how to handle, and Brazil is my exit strategy. Even if Theo hates me at first, he'll get over it while I'm gone. Distance makes it easy to forget.

The door creaks open slowly. Lulu's tiny hand appears holding a chocolate chip cookie. It dances in the air, taunting me. I walk over and pluck it from her hand. She closes the door. The little gesture makes me smile. It also reminds me that I'm not the kind of guy who plays stepdad, and definitely not to my best friend's kid.

"Gio, are you still there?"

"I'm here and I'm still in."

After I end the call, I find Leeyan brushing Lulu's hair in the living room.

"Hey, so we were going to get Thai food."

"Gio likes coconut rice," Lulu informs her.

The little shit is right.

"Great. Let me finish her hair and we'll go. I'm buying," Leeyan insists.

"I can't stay. I have an appointment." I let her think I have a money job.

Her smile disappears, and she stops brushing for a split second.

"Oh." She nods and resumes brushing. "So, that's it then? Things just go back to how they were before?"

Before? Before what? *Before you showed up and fucked me in every way a woman can fuck a man?*

"I need to focus on Brazil."

"I see. Well, I need to focus on this." She keeps brushing.

I tap the side of the door. I really want to punch it because this is so much harder than it should be. Saying goodbye was always the easy part.

"Bye, Gio!" Lulu dismisses me.

"Bye, squirt."

"I'll tell Daddy you came over."

"NO!" Leeyan and I shout, making Lulu jump a little.

Leeyan does damage control. "Gio already called Daddy and told him he stopped by, so you don't have to tell him Gio was here, okay sweetie?"

"Okay." Lulu continues brushing her stuffed elephant. "Can we get ice cream too?"

"Absolutely." Leeyan kisses Lulu's head.

Her eyes meet mine. She's torn. So am I.

As much as I want to make her mine, I know I have to let her go.

CHAPTER SEVENTEEN

My apartment is back to normal: clean, cold, uncluttered. I walk into the kitchen where no less than three dirty dishes sat in the sink at any given time when Leeyan was here. She always had a fresh pot of coffee made, a ball of hair on the bathroom floor, more hair in the shower, on the sofa, and sometimes even on the coffee pot. It was like living with a German Shepherd...an incredibly cute, sexy— *No.* I can't go there.

I've reclaimed some normalcy. I want to keep it that way.

I'm working less side jobs, focusing more on the gym, and prepping for my move. I already spoke to Josie; she's going to call me as soon as she receives a credible offer. A buyer from out of state is interested in the house, sight unseen, and if he turns out to be legit, my parents could be homeless in less than two months. I won't offer them my apartment until the last minute, when they have no choice but to take it.

I walk into rehearsal and drop my bag on an empty chair. All the guys are here—Dain, Rico, Thor, and Theo. Percy is sitting in the corner on his phone, and Ivy is on her laptop pulling up our new music. We're recycling an old cowboy routine to a popular new country song.

"Hey G." Percy is beside me with his hand out.

"What's up?" I take his hand in greeting. "You ready for this?"

He's cocky. "I can do these moves in my sleep. We need to get more inventive."

I must be getting old, because I like our stale routines. "You're lucky to even be here. I wouldn't push my luck." I slap the back of his head. "What's going on with you and your girl?" I'm thirsty for some drama that isn't mine.

"Man, she's trippin." He slaps the air in front of him. "I think she was lying about the baby. After I told her I wouldn't quit—"

I shake my head like *I told you so*.

"Bro, I know. You warned me."

"Look, this life isn't for everyone." I look at Theo doing push-ups with Dain. "Eventually, you'll move on. When the chance comes don't fuck it up."

Percy soaks up every word I say. He thinks I have my shit together, but little does he know we're all hanging on by a thread. Everyone here is one bad decision away from losing it all. That's what life is about—the higher the risk, the better the reward.

"All right, let's get started," Ivy announces.

We spend the next ninety minutes polishing the cobwebs off the old routine. It's only new to Theo and Percy, but Thor is the one struggling. He goes left when we turn right, and he steps on my toes twice. We don't call him Thor for nothing—the guy is a monster with monster-sized feet.

As soon as Ivy calls it for the day, I check my phone. Nothing.

I shouldn't expect anything from Leeyan. We don't owe each other anything. Still, that doesn't mean I can't miss her. For a few weeks, she was my friend, my everything.

I'm a hypocrite.

If the tables were turned, if she were the one desperate to hear from me, that would make her clingy, psycho. What does it make me?

I sit next to Theo because he's the closest thing to Leeyan.

I hand him a bottle of water and ask him about her.

"So, is Leeyan driving you nuts?"

"You know she is." He pulls his boots off.

This is the attitude I always wanted Theo to have when it came to his ex, but instead of saying *I told you so* and launching into a bitch-fest, I want to defend her, want to ask him to cut her a little slack, remind him that she's trying.

"It doesn't help that Dennis let her move into the apartment upstairs."

"At least she can't hear you and Sylvie banging." I'm trying to add in some humor, like the old Gio would do.

"All right, listen up children." Jimmy stands in front of the room and makes an announcement. "Sway's going on the wall."

Making the wall is a big deal, if being a famous stripper is your dream. We congratulate him for making it to the wall of fame inside Trance. He'll be featured on the website and all social media.

Rico sits next to Theo and starts talking about a side job he booked for tonight. If Theo is gone, it might be safe to stop by and see Leeyan.

Am I really that desperate?

I ear-hustle the details just in case I find myself in the neighborhood. The job is a dinner party with a businesswoman, and Rico is trying to explain the required attire.

"Business casual," he says.

"Like khakis and a polo?" Theo has no style.

Rico looks to me for assistance.

"Think Banana Republic," I suggest.

Theo pulls up Google and starts scrolling through ideas.

"This one," Rico says. "You have that blue button-down—wear it with dark jeans and dress shoes. Do you have a sports coat?"

"I have one," I offer. "It's the Gucci one from the fashion show."

I conveniently left it at Leeyan's. Now I have a reason to see her.

"You fucking lifted that?" Rico pretends to be pissed.

"Fuck yeah—they underpaid us." I shove my towel into my bag and stand to leave. "I'll stop by around four." I offer my fist, and Theo hits it.

Rico flips me off.

I text Leeyan and ask her about my coat.

Me: Hey, did I leave a coat at your place?

Leeyan: You mean the one I used to dry my dishes?

Me: Ha. I need to stop by and pick it up tonight. Theo is going to borrow it.

Leeyan: I see how it is now.

I can't tell if she's being sarcastic. I hate texting.

Me: How what is?

Leeyan: You.

Me: What about me?

Leeyan: Are we still friends?

Me: Of course.

My heart pounds. I want to tell her I miss her, tell her the last few weeks have been torture.

Leeyan: Why haven't you called?

Me: I figured you wanted space. You have a lot going on.

She doesn't respond right away. A million reasons go through my mind. Does she want to say more? Does she miss me? Is she using me?

Leeyan: What time are you coming over?

Me: Three-thirty

Leeyan: :)

At three-twenty I pull in front of Theo and Leeyan's building. I double park and run up the front stairs.

"Leeyan," I call out as I open the door.

I hear a man yell, followed by a boom.

I run up the stairs two at a time. When I make it to the top, I see Dennis waddling toward me. He's a short, stubby little fuck.

"What are you doing here?"

He's holding his jaw.

"Where's Leeyan?" I move farther down the hall and look into the living room. Lulu is watching something on a tablet, bright pink headphones covering her ears.

"Are you and Leeyan fucking?" Dennis snaps.

I turn back, ready to throw him down the stairs. I don't care if he owns this building.

"Get out, Dennis." Leeyan appears at the end of the hall with a towel wrapped around her naked body. "Leave now, before I tell him what you did."

I'm frozen. I don't know if I should comfort Leeyan or murder Dennis. I stand between them, waiting to see which way the coin falls.

"Once a whore—"

Dennis doesn't get a chance to finish his sentence. My fist crunches his nose. He stumbles against the wall and I pull back to hit him again. Leeyan grabs my arm, her eyes filled with tears.

"No," she mouths before looking toward the living room.

Lulu.

"Get the fuck out," I hiss. "If I ever see you in this apartment again, you're dead."

Dennis has no smart comeback. He walks into the kitchen and out the back door. I lock it then check on Lulu.

"Hey," I greet her from the doorway.

She looks up and waves then points to the screen. "Little Einstein."

Would she be watching anything else?

I give her a thumbs-up.

Leeyan is already in a pair of jeans and a bra when I walk into the bedroom and close the door.

"Are you okay?" I take her in my arms from behind and inhale her freshly washed hair. It saddens me to find she doesn't smell like Swagger, doesn't smell like me. "What happened? Did he touch you?"

She wiggles out of my arms to put on a black t-shirt. "Is Lulu okay? Did she hear any of that?"

"I don't think so." I wait for her to finish getting dressed before attempting to touch her again. "Can you tell me what happened?"

She turns around with a murderous glare. The strong, angry woman standing a few feet away is trying to keep herself from falling apart. I know whatever happened made her feel weak and it's killing her.

I hesitate to take her hand, but she leaps into my arms. Her breathing is long and deep; she's trying not to cry.

"I was in the shower," she starts. "I thought I heard the bathroom door squeak open and I called Lulu's name. She didn't answer so I kept washing my hair. When I opened my eyes, Dennis was standing there with the curtain open, watching me."

I press her against me, holding her as tight as she's holding me, hanging on to prevent myself from running out the door after Dennis.

"He's been obsessed with me since we were kids. I never thought he'd do something like that."

Dennis was her last resort for a reason. Somewhere deep down, she knew he was a piece-of-shit pervert.

"I'll get a locksmith out here and change the locks." I bet my father can change them himself. Right now, I wish I were handy.

"I decked him pretty hard." She pulls back with a smile. "He won't try anything like that again."

"Yes, well, you still can't stay here."

"This is my only option for now. I need to be close to Lulu."

She pulls me close so I'm holding her again.

"Thank you for being here, Gio."

"There is nowhere in the world I'd rather be."

"Not even Brazil?" she smarts off.

At this moment, no.

"I have to go. I'm supposed to be meeting Theo downstairs to give him my coat. Plus, I'm double parked."

212

"Thank you for being here, Gio." She pulls me close so I'm holding her again.

I lean in to kiss her then stop. "Are we doing this?"

"It's a bad idea, but I'm the queen of bad ideas."

She grabs the front of my shirt and pulls me to her mouth. It's luscious and soft. I nibble her lip and lift her into my arms. Her legs wrap around my waist, and just as I'm about to fall onto the bed, Lulu calls her from the living room.

"Leeyan?"

That little cock-blocker.

I look at her, confused. Leeyan shakes her head and shrugs. We're both clueless as to why Lulu doesn't call her Mom.

"Yeah, baby. Hold on." She adjusts her shirt and tames her hair. "You should probably go."

I don't think Dennis has the balls to come back, but I'd feel better if Leeyan and Lulu were downstairs with me. "Come on, I'll let you into Theo's place. I have a key."

"No, that's weird."

"We'll tell him Lulu wanted to go home and you saw me going into the apartment."

I grab the jacket and give Leeyan my key to Theo's place.

"Here, give him this too." I hand her the Gucci jacket.

I run back to my car and take off, circling the block twice before finding a parking space. Finding parking is a crapshoot. Sometimes you get lucky, and other times you're driving in circles for an hour. My head is spinning from how much has happened in the last ten minutes. I take a few minutes to catch my breath before I get out of the car.

If Leeyan were anyone else in the world, anyone but Theo's ex, it would make my life, my decision easier. For the first time, I want more—more than clothes and money, more than one-night stands. I want to wake up to Leeyan's brown eyes and soft cheeks. I want to smell her in my apartment and make out with her while we wait for the coffee to brew. Hell, I don't even mind having Lulu around. She might be a little cock-blocker, but she's a cool kid.

My phone rings and I answer it on Bluetooth.

"Gio, darling." Antonia's voice booms through my car speakers.

"Antonia," I reply. "How are you?"

"Amazing, darling. I just left your new place. I had furniture set up. You're going to love it!"

"I'm sure I will."

"What's the matter? Something is wrong?"

Everything is wrong. I'm in so deep with these women I'll need a submarine to find my way out.

"I'm driving, shouldn't be on the phone."

"Okay, I won't keep you. I wanted to let you know everything is *perfeito*! I have it all ready for you."

"Perfect." I muster enough false enthusiasm to pacify her for now.

I promise to have a video call this week and disconnect before she has a chance to say goodbye.

What is wrong with me? This is something I've always wanted—running a club, living in Brazil, all of it— but it's turning into a nightmare I can't get out of even if I wanted to. If I bail on Antonia, I won't just lose a job, the deposit on my beachfront apartment, and her friendship; I'll lose my place here, my home—the home I plan to offer my parents.

As I'm walking back to Theo's place, Mom calls.

"Hey Ma, I can't really talk right now."

"The house sold." Her words are harsh and informative. "Josie came by this morning with news of a buyer from Canada. He doesn't care about the mold or the roof. It's a cash offer."

I stop walking. Josie promised to call me if she accepted an offer. "How long do you have?"

"Thirty days."

"How is Dad taking it?"

"He's the same. If we live here or live in China, he's the same."

I end the call but not before she makes me promise to stop by for dinner on Sunday. We only have a handful of meals left in our home. The nostalgia kicks in hard.

I walk into Theo's apartment and smell food, which means one thing—Sylvie is here. *Oh shit.*

"Something smells good," I call out as I open the front door. I told Leeyan to leave it unlocked for me. "Hey Sylvie." I kiss her on the cheek.

She makes a face and motions to where Leeyan is sitting. I pretend to be shocked.

"I made chicken fettuccine. You want to stay for dinner?"

This may be my last meal with them, so of course I agree to stay.

Theo and Leeyan are having a heated exchange when I return to the living room. The last thing she needs right now is more drama. I remind Theo he's running late.

I sit down to eat. Eating is my safe place.

"What's going on?" Sylvie demands. "Does he have a job tonight?" She hesitates to ask in front of Leeyan.

"Rico got a last-minute thing for him." I'm vague too, mainly because I don't want Sylvie to think I'm comfortable in front of Leeyan.

Leeyan is busy listening to Lulu explain the who's who of *Paw Patrol*.

I keep eating.

I eat until Theo returns.

"Good, you're still here. I need a ride."

He looks good in my clothes, and I tell him so as I stand to take my plate to the kitchen. I never make eye contact with Leeyan or acknowledge her presence. I don't want to draw any unnecessary attention to us.

Then I hear Lulu ask if she can call Sylvie "Mommy". The details aren't clear, but I know Leeyan is dying inside. I walk back into the room just as she is running out.

"She's just playing." I fold her into my arms and rub her back.

When I look up, Theo and Sylvie are staring.

Leeyan excuses herself to the bathroom and we leave.

Theo waits until we're in the car to grill me.

"What the fuck was that?"

Knowing I'm leaving for Brazil within weeks relieves some of the pressure of telling Theo. Now that a future with Leeyan is impossible, we can downplay the present.

"Nothing, bro. We're friends."

"I saw you walk into her apartment earlier."

Fuck. Fuck. Fuck.

"It isn't what you think. She needed to talk one night and we kind of became friends." I consider telling him about her staying at the Green Tortoise. I could lie, could say I ran into her at the cheesesteak place. It could've happened, but it will lead to more questions.

"What do you guys *talk* about?" He air-quotes the word "talk". He knows me—the old Gio didn't talk.

"You," I answer, being honest for once—almost. "She feels horrible about leaving." I don't want to push too far in her favor, but he needs to know she's sorry and deserves a second chance.

My words fall on deaf ears. He warns me to be careful.

"Leeyan only cares about Leeyan."

You're wrong. You don't know her the way I do.

"I'm good, bro." I hold out my fist, the one that just socked Dennis less than an hour ago. "Hit me up later if you need a ride."

I peel away from the curb and drive straight home, where I sit down at my desk and call Josie. She sends the call the voicemail, and the message I leave is not nice. Guilt leads me to my go-to. I warm up my mom's eggplant parmesan, even though I already ate dinner. It doesn't matter since I'm going to puke it up later anyway, along with my pride.

CHAPTER EIGHTEEN

After I vomit and rinse, I decide to pack.

I look around my apartment and consider what I need to take with me to Brazil: my clothes, the little jewelry I own, and my laptop.

Everything else is bullshit.

Leeyan left for the army with nothing, and she came back with nothing—to nothing. What will be my reason for coming back?

The furniture, the art, even my car—I don't need anything of those things to survive. They aren't worth returning for. When it comes down to it, I don't want them.

I want her.

The phone near the door rings. It can only be Fred.

"Mr. Castillo, you have a guest." Fred thinks it's funny when he announces my visitors this way. "Shall I send her up?"

"Who is it?"

"It's your houseguest, and she brought a friend."

I'm confused. Does he mean Leeyan?

"I'm coming down."

I slip into my sneakers and put on a hoodie, zipping it to hide my bare chest. When the elevator doors open, I hear the voice of someone I know. Someone little.

"Gio." Lulu waves. "This is your house?"

What the hell?

"No, this is a lobby." I pull Leeyan to the side. "What are you doing here?"

She looks hurt and lost. "I didn't have anywhere else to go." Her voice is shaky. She's been crying. "This wasn't planned. It just kind of happened."

"Does Theo know you're here?"

She shakes her head while Lulu giggles at something Fred is showing her on his phone. He does a great job of keeping her occupied.

"Sylvie left the room and I went into fight-or-flight mode."

"More like flight." I gesture to the bags on the floor. "What is this, Leeyan? Did you take Lulu?"

"Yes." She builds a little steam. "She's my daughter— I have rights too. We don't have a custody agreement. I looked it up, and she can live with me."

"Where is all this coming from?" I remember what happened with Dennis. Leeyan is spiraling, and when she gets like this, she runs.

"I have an offer to work in Alameda for the sheriff's department. They have a program for ex-military, and the job pays well. I'll be able to give her a good life."

"Her life is here, with Theo."

She shakes her head. "I don't know why I thought you would understand. You're on his side."

"I'm on no side. This isn't my—"

"Problem," she finishes my sentence. "I'm not your problem." She spins away and grabs the bags. "Let's go, Lulu."

I don't stop her when she picks up Lulu and walks out the door.

"Youngblood," Fred calls. "You all right?"

"No, not even close."

I take the stairs up to my apartment. I'm drenched in sweat and my heart is racing. Do I call Theo? Do I call the police?

I should go after Leeyan, help her.

Help her do what? Kidnap Lulu? No.

I can't let her do this.

I can't let her fuck this up.

She came to me because she trusts me. I have to at least hear her out.

I race back downstairs and onto the street. She's standing on the corner, looking down at her phone. Lulu clings to her leg.

This is my moment, that moment in a book when the good guy rescues the girl. I plan what I'm going to say as I walk up behind her. Confess my feelings. Tell her she deserves a happy ending and I am the man to give it to her.

I stop short to catch my breath before tapping her shoulder. Just as I open my mouth to say her name, Lulu speaks.

"I have to poop."

"Can you hold it just a little longer?" Leeyan asks as she taps her phone. I see the Uber app on her screen.

"I think it's a big one."

Leeyan looks up and finally notices me standing behind her.

"You scared the shit out of me!" she yells.

"You almost scared the poop of me too!" Leeyan dances in place. "Mommy..."

"You can use my bathroom." I scoop Lulu into my arms and race back up to my apartment.

I set her down in front of the bathroom door. "You're all good...you can do this alone?"

"Duh." She rolls her eyes—Leeyan's eyes.

Leeyan is settling on the sofa. Her phone rings, and she quickly declines the call.

"Thanks for that." She points to the hall where her daughter is taking a dump in my pristine toilet.

I sit down and put my arm around her. "Come here."

She slides closer and rests her head on my shoulder. "I fucked up, but I can't go back. As soon as I walk into my apartment, I feel his eyes on me."

"You need to file a report on him. I don't give a fuck if he owns the building." I'm about to offer my place when I remember I'm already giving it to my parents.

"I have nowhere to go. If I lose that apartment, I'm on the street. I don't have enough money to afford a place in the city, and the thought of living far away from Lulu kills me."

She presses her hand to my chest.

I know the feeling.

"I'm leaving soon—sooner than I thought."

She moves out of my arms. "Brazil?"

"Yeah. My parents' house sold. They have thirty days, and I worked it out so they can stay here. I have a place waiting for me in Rio and nothing really holding me here. You can stay until my parents move in. That should buy you some time to figure out your next move."

She moves away from me on the couch. "You have nothing holding you here?" I sense pain in her tone. "What about me? Us?"

"It will never work out," I reason.

She desperately grabs the front of my hoodie and forces me to look her in the eyes. "Then let's fail together."

At this moment, I have never wanted to fail harder. I won't risk my future, Leeyan's relationship with Lulu, or Theo's feelings. This is bigger than her and me. Leeyan's phone rings; it's Theo. So many lives are affected by our actions.

"Answer it before he calls the police."

I leave to check on Lulu.

"Everything good in there?"

How long does it take for a kid her size to take a shit?

The door opens, and Lulu walks out. "You have nice soap."

I look at the sink, which is covered in suds.

Leeyan raises her voice in the living room, so I suggest we go into my room. I turn on the TV.

Lulu jumps climbs onto the bed and kicks off her shoes. "Do you have *Paw Patrol?*"

"Uh, I don't know." I click a few buttons to try to search for it.

"I can do it." Lulu holds her hand out for the remote.

I give it to her then tell her I'll be back.

Leeyan is agreeing to go home when I return to the room.

"Did you work it out?"

"Yeah, for now." She walks into my arms. "I can't do this without you."

Holding her is like a long exhale. I close my eyes and enjoy the feeling while I can.

***

I wait in my car around the corner while Leeyan delivers Lulu back to Theo. A few minutes later, she comes storming down the street. I honk so she knows where I am.

"He lied!" She starts rambling about revenge and getting back at him. "I will fucking end him!"

I can't listen to her make threats about Theo. He's my best friend. If I have to choose a side, life forces me to pick him.

"I should just leave. It will make everyone's life easier."

"How did that work out for you last time?"

She shakes her head and sighs. "I fucked up and now he's going to use this against me. Fight or flight..."

"You fight for what you want. Leaving never solved anything." I eat my words. "If you stay and fight for Lulu, I'll stay and support you."

What am I saying?

This is not how you make life decisions. This is irrational and emotional...and it feels so right.

"I won't get between you and Theo. I can't talk about it with you or listen to you criticize him. Theo is a great father, and he has never done anything to prove otherwise."

Leeyan nods. "You'll stay? For me?"

"For us."

Leeyan is my future, but the road happily ever after is bumpy, and complicated, and requires a lot of whiskey. I won't stand on either side of a courtroom and watch the two people I care about most in the world rip each other apart. I can't take that journey with her; she has to do it alone.

CHAPTER NINETEEN

I call Josie three times to apologize for my first message. I reach her on my fourth try. She apologizes for not calling me first and invites me over for coffee.

"It's a cash offer. He's motivated and ready to buy."

"Josie, I want the house." I pull an envelope from my pocket. "You said you'd give me the option of matching your best offer."

"You can afford the mortgage?"

"I can make it work."

I already applied to three boutiques in Union Square. It's time to take my knowledge of high fashion to the next level. With what I make at Trance, I can swing it.

"The down payment?"

I slide a cashier's check across her dining room table.

She looks at the check and shakes her head. "I have to tell you, I'm surprised." She points at me in a good way. "You surprised me, Giovanni. I told Mags you were one of the good ones."

"Do we have a deal?"

"I'll co-sign the mortgage, that way if you get into any trouble I can help you. And I get the house back if you default."

"You'll do that for me?"

"I told you I wanted to keep the house in the family."
She stands, and I reach out to shake her hand. She slaps it away.

"Come here." She holds her arms open. "I'm so proud of you. Do your parents know?"

"No, I want to surprise them."

"Oh, they will be!"

***

I decide to wait until we close on the house to tell my parents I'm their new landlord. I'm petrified at what my father is going to say. After breaking the news to Antonia, nothing phases me.

She cursed me for twenty minutes straight. Threatened to kick me out of my apartment. Called me every curse word imaginable in English and Portuguese. At the end of it all, she settled for Rico.

He was more than happy to take my place in Brazil. After all the shit he gave me about moving, it all boiled down to jealousy. When I offered him the chance to take my place, he jumped at it. He's been there a month and texts me every day to thank me for being a pussy.

I walk into my parent's house—my house—and yell hello. Boxes are stacked from the front door all the way down the hall. I waited too long to tell them. They're all packed and ready to go. Where I have no clue.

"Giovanni." Dad appears from the kitchen. "I need a hand." I follow him into the kitchen and find the sink in pieces.

"What are you doing?"

"The drain is slow. I don't want anyone accusing me of being lazy."

"That's ridiculous, dad. Just leave it." I calculate how much this is going to cost me. "I'll call a plumber."

"What for? I'm almost done." He lays on his back, halfway under the kitchen sink. "Hold the faucet, don't let it turn."

I straddle his legs and reach over to grab the faucet. It moves slightly.

"Don't let it move!" Dad yells.

"I didn't." I grip it tighter.

He grunts a few more times before announcing he's done. He stands and elbows past me.

"See." He turns on the water, it sputters out. I watch it swirl around the sink, then down the drain. "See."

"It only took you fourteen years to fix it." Mom kills his thunder. She greets me with a kiss on the cheek. "You hungry?"

"No, thanks. What's with all the boxes?"

"We're moving," she says. "You know this."

I never offered my apartment, they don't know I bought the house, where could they possibly be going?

"Did you find a new place?" I follow mom out of the kitchen, into my old room.

"Yes." She doesn't offer any other information. "Do you need sheets? I have so many sheets."

"No, I don't need sheets. Where are you moving?"

"Josie gave us a deal on a place in San Anselmo. It's darling. You should come see it."

I should come see it? Josie got them a place? Why didn't she mention this when I was handing her my life's savings?

"Josie rented you a house in San Anselmo? How will dad get to work?" San Anselmo is on the Marin side of the bay. It's one hell of a commute over the Golden Gate Bridge.

"Your father is retired. His last day was Friday. He's a free man."

"I don't know about free," Dad chimes in from behind me. "Where's the tape? I need to make a box."

"Living room table," Mom says. "Bring it here when you're finished."

I watch my parents pack their things in bewilderment. They look happy. "How much is Josie charging you to rent the place?"

"We bought the house, hot shot," Dad says as he walks away. "What are you writing a book."

"No, but I do think I'm entitled to know what is going on. I thought you were broke." Reality begins to sink in.

I bought this house for nothing.

"Who said we're broke?" Mom looks offended.

"I assumed since you didn't buy this house...you couldn't afford it."

"Your father has a good retirement. He was union, you know, and I didn't want this house. I want to live in the country, with a garden and sun more than ten times a year." Mom stacks at least ten sets of sheets on the bed. "The new house is small, for two people, maybe three." She looks at me in that way moms do. "In case you settle down, have kids."

230

I think of Leeyan. We're on a break while she deals with the custody battle. By break, I mean we only see each other once a week. I can't hold out any longer than that. I also can't choose a side. The line was drawn between her and Theo and I refuse to cross it. I'm Switzerland.

I blamed a lot of my actions on my father. His lack of respect and support was like a hall pass. I made choices under the impression that nobody cared about the man I was becoming. It wasn't until Leeyan slithered back into my life that I began to care. I want to be a better man for her and for me.

"What are you doing with all this stuff, ma?"

"Donating it. Some I'm giving to Maggie. She likes this desk."

I blush.

"Josie said the new owner might want some of the old furniture. I don't know," she shrugs. "What kind of person wants this old stuff."

"The kind who lost his ass on this house. For what they paid, they need anything they can take." Dad sets the tape on the desk. "Nice desk, huh Theo?" he chuckles at my expense.

I walk out of the room. Everywhere I turn there are boxes. Boxes filled with useless crap. We accumulate so much crap in our lives. In the end, it's worthless. Even this house. My parents don't need to live here to be happy. This place is their home because it's where they live. Being together is what makes them happy.

"Do you think the new owner will want the dining room table? It doesn't fit the new house?" Mom runs her hand along the polished cherry wood.

"Yes." I sit in my chair. "I'll keep it. And the hutch." I point to the matching cabinet.

"You? This fits in your apartment?" Mom looks at me curiously.

"No. But it fits here. This table belongs in this house. No matter who lives here."

"Do you think it's a family?" Mom wipes a smudge with her apron. "It's a good house to raise a family.

Yes. It is.

CHAPTER TWENTY

"Daddy said you were his best friend and now you're my mommy's best friend."

"Was he smiling when he told you this?"

Theo and I haven't really hashed out the how and when I ended up with Leeyan. We're all adjusting to the new custody agreement. It's been a long year, but I see the light at the end of the tunnel.

"I don't know." Lulu shrugs. "Is it true?"

"Sort of."

I go back to buttering bread, and her little eyes burn through the back of my head. She's waiting for a longer explanation. "I'm still your dad's best friend."

"But now you love my mommy."

"Whoa. No need to drop the L-word."

"Daddy used to be best friends with Sylvie then they fell in love."

"Yeah, well I'm not your daddy."

Harsh.

"Do you want to be?" She pauses and reflects on the dumbfounded expression I'm sporting. "Do you want to have a baby with my mommy like Sylvie and Daddy?"

"This may be difficult for your young brain to comprehend, but not everyone in the world wants to be Sylvie and your daddy."

"Duh." She rolls her little eyes at me. "If you and Mommy get married that means your mommy and daddy will be my grandma and grandpa."

I smile at this because my parents love Lulu. Mom cries every time she comes over and sees my old room decked out in *Paw Patrol* décor.

The phone on the wall rings. I kept my parents' old landline; it's been their number forever, and I didn't want to give it up.

Lulu runs to answer it. "Hello?" Her eyes light up. "I was just telling Gio he should marry my mommy so I can call you Grandpa!"

I take the phone before she spills any more tea.

"Hey Pop." I pull the cord and walk back to the stove. I place the bread in the pan and top the slices with cheese.

"Your mother left a box of Christmas crap in the garage. You going to be home Saturday?"

"You have a key, Dad. You can come by anytime."

Once my parents found out I bought the house and my mother stopped crying, I asked them to stay, but they had their hearts set on moving to the cottage. They had no problem, however, leaving the garage full of things they couldn't take with them but didn't have the heart to throw away, like old holiday decorations.

"We want to see you and Lulu."

Lulu is like a goodwill ambassador; her presence creates peace between my father and me. Buying the house and committing to Leeyan didn't hurt either. I have a feeling Dad likes me now. He's just too stubborn to admit it.

"She'll be with Theo Saturday."

Lulu pulls the cord until I turn around. "I want to see Mr. Alberto!" she whines.

"Okay, shh." I pull the cord out of her hands and flip her grilled cheese. "We'll see."

"It's going to rain next week so I need to show you how to clear the gutters." Dad likes to show me things around the house.

I let him explain how the breaker box works and what to do if the pilot light on the water heater goes out. I made some improvements before moving in. The kitchen and bathrooms were updated. I let Dad choose the paint for the living room. Spending hours in Home Depot together was a bonding experience. Shopping for paint brushes and masking tape gave me insight about my father.

Over the years, he made small repairs and painted the shutters. Those tasks were favors for Josie, not improvements to his home. Dad resented my career choice because he wanted me to be a better man. Have more than he could provide for his family. When I told him I bought the house, his perception of me changed. I can't pinpoint it or even see the transformation. I hear the pride in his voice.

"Sure, Dad. I'll see you Saturday. I have to finish making Lulu dinner."

"Gio?"

"Yeah?"

"You did good."

Oh yeah, he definitely likes me.

I place the phone on the cradle and Lulu drums her fingers on the white marble counter.

"Do you want a sandwich or what?"

"Yes, but no—"

"Crust, got it."

I trim the edges and set the plate in front of her.

"What are you guys up to?" Leeyan sits on the empty stool next to Lulu. She inspects the crust-less grilled cheese and steals a bite. "That's yummy. I want one."

I pull two pieces of bread from the bag and butter them.

"That's the best-grilled cheese ever. Don't you think, Lulu?"

She's overdoing it.

"It's all right." Lulu shrugs. "I like mine with Havarti."

"Havarti?" I snort.

"She has a very sophisticated pallet," Leeyan says in her defense. "I can thank Sylvie for that at least."

"Sylvie has food challenges so Reese will try new things. He's picky. I'm not picky. I try all the things."

"Most boys are picky   ," Leeyan replies in a *sorry to tell you this* kind of way.

Lulu nibbles her sandwich then looks at me. "Are you picky, Gio?"

"Depends on what we're talking about."

"Gio is the exception." Leeyan gives me a sideways glance. "He isn't like the other boys."

"That's why you love him right, Mommy?"

For the love of Pete.

"I have to go." Leeyan kisses the top of Lulu's head. "You're still good with taking her to school in the morning?" She wraps her arms around my waist as I flip over her grilled cheese.

"Yep, we're all set." I remove the sandwich from the pan and place it on a paper towel. "Here's your dinner to-go."

Leeyan is on nights, which means I get to spend two nights a week alone with Lulu. Theo could veto this, but he doesn't. That's how I know everything will be all right.

I walk her to the front door and help with her gear. She puts on her holster then her jacket. Her army friend was able to pull a lot of strings and get her into a police department closer to home. It's a little beach city fifteen minutes out of San Francisco.

"Be safe, Mommy." Lulu watches us from the doorway of the kitchen, the same doorway with the notches recording my height from ages five to fifteen. I refused to let Mom measure me after that, because I was an asshole.

"Thank you, baby. Be a good girl for Gio. Let him pick a movie too." She shrugs into her jacket as her partner pulls up to the house.

"But I'm so sick of Twilight," Lulu whines.

"Hey, it was a marathon," I explain. "One day you'll thank me."

"I doubt it," she sasses and then returns to the kitchen.

Leeyan gets serious when I try to kiss her goodbye.

"About last night..." she starts.

"I was drunk."

"Liar."

"I was in the moment, and it just slipped out." I kiss her before she has a chance to reply. "You're going to be late." I open the door and wave to Chad, her partner.

"You're the one who told me you weren't ready to play stepdad. What did you say? You weren't finished being selfish."

"It sounds really bad when you say it."

At the time, right after the custody battle, I meant it.

She kisses me on the chin. "Are you done selfishly making my daughter dinner and taking care of her when I'm at work?" She kisses my neck.

"I'm done pretending we're just playing house."

She throws her arms around me, but all I feel is her bulletproof vest.

"Are you drunk right now?"

"Nope."

"Does this mean you love me?"

I take her face in my hands and look into her pretty brown eyes.

"Baby, I'm so in love with you."

We kiss. It's soft and sexy. It's the kind of kiss you give the woman you love.

Chad honks.

Fucker.

"I have to go." She folds the paper towel around her sandwich. "Have you considered going to culinary school? You really are a great cook."

This is her not-so-subtle way of telling me I need to get a new job. She's been dropping hints for weeks.

"I think Costco is hiring," I joke.

"I'm all about buying in bulk." She squeezes my bicep then walks out the door.

And just like that, my career at Trance is over.

Many thanks...

It took a lot of snacking and drinking to create Giovanni's story. Thank you to my family who lived on pizza and frozen mac & cheese. F-U to the IRS who decided to audit me!

To the members of Nicole's Book Rehab:
Thanks for keeping your notifications on.
This book is for you.

To the ladies who read this before it was perfect:
Lee: Thank you for dedicating your time & patience.
Praise be.
Rachel: I'm not going to thank you for making me do the work I didn't want to do. Or for reading three drafts of the same chapters. I don't even know why I listen to you. Next time I'll listen to my gut, which apparently, is where you dwell.

To the beta readers who received the first draft
SORRY!

C. Marie:
Thank so much for squeezing me in last minute.
You rock!

Last, but not least...
To my dog – Achilles.
You smell. You don't listen. And you snore. But I love the hell out of you. Even though I yell and tell you to shut up when you bark and the wind. I appreciate every day I have left with you.

NEED MORE MEN OF TRANCE?

Read Theo's story now!
Sneak peek in the back of this book.

This isn't the end.
More to come from Rico and Dain!

Don't miss out - Join my Facebook
Group Nicole's Book Rehab

Don't forget to leave a review on
Goodreads and Amazon!

Chapter One

Most of my parenting skills were derived from animated sitcoms and Adam Sandler movies. Since my father rarely made an appearance in my life; guys like Homer Simpson and Peter Griffin became my mentors. I've never strangled my daughter or attempted to run her over with the car, and yet, I'd still take second place to Homer for father of the year.

Because one: I can't afford a car.

And two: I don't have a killer job in a nuclear facility that probably offers an excellent benefits package.

Fatherhood has been a learn-as-you-go experience for me. I can't tell you how many times I wrapped my daughter in a t-shirt and plastic bag because I forgot to buy diapers. Or fed her fish-shaped crackers and apple juice for dinner. And maybe, just maybe, Lulu's first word was shit.

Could've been sit or spit.

Tonight, I'm upping my game. I'm going full Mike Brady. Minus the suit and tie. Minus clothes period.

If there is one thing television has taught me; it's this:

Good fathers make sacrifices.

Whether it's giving up on your dream to play professional baseball or shaving all your body hair, good dads provide a better life for the people they love. Believe it or not, there are men in this world who put their children first. I've never actually met one of these unicorns, but I'm pretty sure they exist. If things work out with my new job; I'll be shitting rainbows by the end of the month.

I turn off the shower, pull a towel from the silver bar on the wall, and perform a sniff test. I try to hit the laundry mat once a week, but when you have to decide between clean towels and eating; a case of ramen noodles wins every time.

The struggle is real. But it won't last forever. Not if I can help it. One day I'll have so many fresh fucking towels I'll need a closet to hold them all.

Goals.

Goals are good.

Clean towels are even better.

I wrap the funky smelling towel around my waist and open the bathroom door to find my only reason for living sitting in the hallway.

"Why are you sitting in the hall, Lulu?" I step over a line of stuffed animals. "It's too dark; you're gonna ruin your eyes."

I don't know if that's true, but I'm pretty sure I heard it somewhere. "Go sit in the front room."

"Okay, Daddy." She gathers her animal audience and shuffles down the hall.

Lulu is a smart kid, and I'm not saying that because she's mine. Lulu's preschool teacher thinks she has a highly developed intellect and recommended her to a private school in the Mission District. I'm a public-school kid; I take pride in that. I assumed Lulu would go to my old school, you know, follow the tradition.

When I told Lulu's teacher my plan, she made a face. Since I have no fucking clue what I'm doing, I feed off the reactions of people that do. That face told me I was an idiot.

I took a tour of the Elite Institute and right off the bat, you know this place is special. The kids sit on bean bag chairs or pillows, wherever they feel comfortable. No assigned seating. That blew me away. Until I saw the desks, not desks, workstations with ergonomically correct chairs. It looked more like a fancy tech company than a kindergarten class.

Man, you should've seen Lulu's eyes when we walked into the library. She couldn't wipe the smile from her face. At the end of the tour, I let Lulu take the entrance test, and of course, she aced it. That's when they hit me with the price. Just like a good car salesman.

Twenty grand.

That's for one year. Not even a year, nine months.

I know what you're thinking, twenty G's so kids can finger paint, but it's more than that. This is the kind of place that churns out CEO's, and shit. I want to give Lulu every advantage to make it in this ruthless world. So, if you were wondering why I shaved all the hair off my body, that's why.

I check my duffel to make sure I have deodorant and a clean towel. Two things Giovanni told me never to forget. I zip the bag and look in the mirror. I'm not normally this narcissistic, but I've never been this cut. It took two months, six containers of weight-gainer, and countless hours in the gym to get here. I don't think I've ever worked this hard for anything. My last job was picking up shit at a doggy daycare. That didn't require any brain cells, let alone muscle.

I've had ten jobs in the three years since Leeyan left for the army. While she's off finding herself, I'm here doing whatever is necessary to make sure our daughter has a halfway decent life. I'm not asking for any awards. I know women have been doing this very same thing for centuries.

I wish Leeyan were one of them.

Everything seemed great on the surface. The problem with living on the surface is that sometimes you miss a step and fall into a hole. Leeyan fell about six months after Lulu was born. You can call it postpartum depression or whatever, but deep down I knew she didn't want to be a mother. Leeyan had just enlisted when we met. Knowing we'd only be together for two months made every moment went spent together more intense and meaningful. We kissed deeper, laughed harder. I didn't think I'd fall in love with her. I really tried to avoid it, but Leeyan isn't the kind of woman you can love casually. It's all or nothing with her, and I went all in.

The morning she placed the pregnancy test on the table next to my bowl of Lucky Charms; luck was the furthest thing from my mind. I didn't have the best childhood, Leeyan lost both of her parents when she was young. My parents exist somewhere in the world; they just aren't part of mine. I prefer it that way.

We swore our daughter would have more and we would do better. Leeyan might have bailed on our plan, but I'm going to see it through no matter what.

The doorbell rings and Lulu's little footsteps run towards the hall.

"Check the window first," I remind her.

I have a little peephole set up in the window beside the door so she can look out without the person on the porch seeing her. We live in a renovated flat across the street from Dolores Park. It's a safe neighborhood, but you never know who might knock on your door. I'm not exactly ducking my landlord, but I don't want to see the guy right now. Rent was due two days ago, and I'm a little light. I need this job to work out, not just for Lulu's tuition. My building is owned, was owned, by Leeyan's godmother. She passed away seven months ago and her son, Dennis, took over. The guy is a first-class prick. Leeyan thinks of him as a brother. To Dennis, she's the star of all his wet dreams.

"It's Sylvie!" Lulu announces, and I hear the lock click open.

Sylvie is babysitting for me tonight. I wouldn't be able to do this without her.

I put on a white v-neck Polo shirt and jeans. Gio says I should dress casually to and from the club. It's best to keep a low profile. I slide on a belt then sit on the bed to put on my Jordan's. This is the kind of thing I wear when I go grocery shopping with Lulu or to grab a drink with the guys. To Giovanni, it's low-key, but it's the nicest outfit I own.

I stand before the mirror and check off my list.

Hair: My fade is on point.

Face: Moisturized and clear of blemishes. My blue eyes glow beneath my newly shaped eyebrows.

Body: I won't go into detail, but my abs belong on the cover of Men's Health. I'm just shy of six feet, but those few inches I lack in height were put to good use in the other areas.

Yeah, I'm feeling myself a little right now. When you've worked as hard as I have, a little vanity is understandable. I've transformed my dad bod into a sex god.

I walk into the living room and find Sylvie bent over picking up crayons. We had a friends-with-benefits thing happening before she met Aaron. After that, we became friends sans the benefits.

"Hey, you," I say and try not to look at her ass.

Sylvie looks up and slightly gasps at my appearance. She recovers quickly and pretends I don't look like a stud.

"Hey," she says as she picks up her son. "Say hi," she coaxes Reese. He looks at me and continues fisting his mouth as Sylvie places him in Lulu's old baby saucer.

We don't have much furniture, just a crappy IKEA couch and a table holding a 42-inch flat screen. Most of Lulu's baby stuff is still set up; taking it down will make the room feel empty.

"You ready?" She tilts her head and searches for something to criticize. I'm flawless right now, on the outside at least.

"Ready as I'll never be." I squat down to kiss Lulu and look down Sylvie's top. I don't mean to be a perv, but hell. She's wearing a baggy V-neck t-shirt. I can tell by the outline of her tits that she isn't wearing a bra. Not that she needs one. Even full of breastmilk, her tits are stellar.

"I love you, Lulu." I kiss her head, and she stands up. "Bedtime is eight, don't forget to brush your teeth."

"I know, Daddy. Good luck at your new work."

I lift her into my arms and smell her freshly washed hair. When it's still damp, like now, and smells like coconut and flowers—it's my favorite smell in the world. I want to tell her how much I love her. How I'll do anything for her. Unlike Leeyan, I put Lulu before my happiness, my dignity. When Leeyan was here, she did all the things a mother should, but there was no joy in it. Lulu deserves better than a mother who treats her like a chore.

"Come on, sweetie, let Daddy go to work." Lulu unwraps her arms and legs from around me and moves into Sylvie's arms. "Be a good girl while I give your daddy a present. She kisses my daughter then sets her on the floor.

"Did you say present?" I clap like a tween girl as we walk across the hall into the kitchen. It's a little room with a small refrigerator and stove. Leeyan found the red Formica table and black-and-white chairs at a garage sale. It looks like the fifties threw up in here.

Sylvie reaches into her purse and hands me a matte black can. "It's your first bottle of man-spray."

"Syl, I don't know how to thank you." I press the can to my chest. "We're having a moment."

Sylvie flips me off. "Just make sure you avoid the face, everywhere else is fair game." Her eyes dip to my crotch and back.

The bottle says Tom Ford Oud Wood and looks expensive.

"You need your own scent;" she explains.

"What was your scent?"

Sylvie cringes whenever I ask her about dancing. She worked at a club for three years and didn't go back after Reese was born. She's in phlebotomy school now, and works part time at a nail salon. Most of her income is from Reese's father. The guy hasn't seen his son in a month, but he never misses a child support payment.

"If I was on stage I usually sprayed on some cheap Bath & Body crap. When I worked the floor, I brought out the big guns. Gucci, Dior."

Smell is the strongest sense linked to memory. All I had to do was a get a whiff of Sylvie's perfume, and I'd get hard.

"What was the one I liked?"

"Gucci Bamboo." She kind of shudders. "Ever since I was pregnant with Reese, the smell of that makes me yak."

Leeyan was the same way when she was pregnant. It's like her nose was on a higher frequency. She could smell one of Giovanni's blunts on my clothes as soon as I walked through the door.

"Thanks, Sylvie. For this." I hold up the bottle. "For everything." She's my go-to whenever I need a sitter, a recipe, a break.

"Just give me a hug, and we'll call it even." She wraps her arms around my waist. Most girls go for the neck, not Sylvie. She's a waist hugger. "I can do without sex, but hugs are a necessity." She moans softly into my chest.

"Definitely." I enjoy her body pressed to mine for a few seconds before letting go. I always break away first.

"Remember," Sylvie pokes me in the chest, "those cute little hipster bitches are just there to have fun. Take their money and come home."

"Yes, Mother." I walk out of the kitchen and pick up my duffel. Sylvie already gave me an earful when I told her I got a job at the club. She warned me about balance and drawing lines. People make stupid decisions when money is on the table or the floor.

"For real, Theo. Keep your head in the game."

I open the door and turn around with one of my sexy stares. She pulls lower lip with her teeth and looks at me like she wants to lick the icing off my cake. I like that I still get to her. Feeling wanted gets me off. What can I say, I'm a dude.

"I got this, Sylvie."

I open the door and walk out almost convinced that my positive attitude is real. I'm scared as shit of failing.

The pressure is so real.

I walk through the park towards the train. A group of girls no older than fifteen is sitting on a blanket, passing a pink S'well bottle around. One of them has long dark hair and blue eyes. She's wearing a Mission High School hoodie. My alma mater. She is Lulu ten years from now. Sitting in the park on a Friday night drinking with her friends because that's what public school kids do for fun. I'm not saying kids that go to private school wouldn't steal a bottle of their parent's wine and or do a little Addy to stay up all night playing Scrabble. I want to believe educated kids have better ways to entertain themselves.

Smart kids equal smart choices.

If I want Lulu to have a fighting chance, that starts with the Elite Institute. If sending to her a hipster school means I have to dress like a cowboy and swing my rope for a room full of drunk women; then yee-fucking-haw.

About the Author

Want to know more about Nicole?

Check out her social media:

Instagram: @nicoleloufas

Twitter: @nicoleloufas

Facebook: Nicole Loufas, Author

Join my Facebook group: Nicole's Book Rehab

Visit her website: www.nicoleloufas.com